Moving Forward

Lisa Wilford

Moving Forward

I hope you enjoyed my book! Thank you for supporting me —
Lisa Wilford
xoxo

Vanguard Press

VANGUARD PAPERBACK

© Copyright 2024
Lisa Wilford

The right of Lisa Wilford to be identified as author of this work has been asserted by her in accordance with the Copyright, Designs and Patents Act 1988.

All Rights Reserved

No reproduction, copy or transmission of this publication may be made without written permission.
No paragraph of this publication may be reproduced, copied or transmitted save with the written permission of the publisher, or in accordance with the provisions of the Copyright Act 1956 (as amended).

Any person who commits any unauthorized act in relation to this publication may be liable to criminal prosecution and civil claims for damages.

A CIP catalogue record for this title is available from the British Library.

ISBN 978 1 80016 956 2

This is a work of fiction. Names, characters, businesses, places, events and incidents are either the product of the author's imagination or used in a fictitious manner. Any resemblance to actual persons, living or dead, or actual events is purely coincidental.

Vanguard Press is an imprint of
Pegasus Elliot Mackenzie Publishers Ltd.
www.pegasuspublishers.com

First Published in 2024

Vanguard Press
Sheraton House Castle Park
Cambridge England

Printed & Bound in Great Britain

Everyone has a dream and dreams do come true.

I could not have begun this creative journey without the encouragement, support, and guidance of Cynthia Gurin of QuantumCat.com editing.

Chapter One

The Beginning... Sort of

As casual biker bars go, the one owned by Big Lou would probably rank in the top ten percent for its part of North Carolina. You could find at least a hundred bikes in the dirt and gravel parking lot at any given time, and for good reasons. The place was clean, the beer was ice cold, the drinks were strong, and the food was hearty and cheap. Folks who frequented the place were generally friendly, there were plenty of pool tables, there was a juke box that blasted music during the day and a decent band belted out live music at night. A couple of stripper poles had been mounted on top of the bar, installed mostly as a joke, but frisky female stripper wannabes were welcome, and they always earned a big hand.

It looked like a dump, of course. A sprawling old flat-roof weather-beaten frame building, reminiscent of a B-grade Western movie set. The façade boasted a six by twelve-foot covered porch slapped on the front as an afterthought some fifty years earlier, and whatever paint the building might once have benefited from had long since peeled off. An assortment of Harley and beer signs haphazardly festooned the exterior, accurately setting expectations for the interior.

A vintage orange neon sign proclaiming *saloon* was mounted atop the rickety covered entry porch and broadcast a permanent bzzzzzttttt sound when it got dark, and somebody eventually remembered to switch it on. The sign threw off just enough of a glow to keep patrons from tripping.

Big Lou made folks feel welcome, so by and large everybody thought the place was pretty much perfect.

***

The sleek black Harley Electra Glide pulled smoothly into the mostly dirt and gravel parking lot and the driver, John Thompson, cut the engine. He had thoughtfully chosen the only section of the lot that still had a worn asphalt patch which led to the front door. He pulled off his helmet, ran a hand through his hair and spoke over his shoulder to the pillion passenger.

"I just need to touch base with Bobby Murphy for a minute, Sarah, he's got a real estate contract he wants me to look over before he signs it. I'll be maybe five minutes max, and then we can be on our way."

His passenger, Sarah Watson, raised her arms to lift off the Bell full face helmet, then casually shook out a shoulder-length waterfall of natural blonde hair. She grabbed his waist to steady herself as she dismounted, then waited for the owner of the bike to lock it.

"Take your time," she smiled. Their plans were fluid and they weren't going far, just a party at a mutual friend's place a half-mile down the road, and the bar was a stop along on the way. She hadn't even bothered to wear a jacket.

He joined her and smiled back, mischief on his mind. Day-yum but this woman was smokin' hot. Black tank top, tight black jeans, red stiletto heels. Hoo-boy.

A blast of cool, liquor-scented air and a pounding beat from the juke box as it switched from the toe-tapping redneck rhythm to a selection of vintage rock greeted them as they walked through the door. The bar's patrons were an eclectic mix of rednecks, weekend bikers and serious bikers. They were eating, drinking, shooting pool, playing penny-ante poker, slamming vintage pinball machines, and a handful were on the dance floor.

The pair of women working the busy bar today were a study in contrasts. Karen was an affable, busty bleached blonde. She wore a polka dot bathing suit bottom along with a strapless lace bra which had partially teased its way out of a beribboned navy tank top, allowing a fair amount of her bosomy bounty to overflow. Karen knew how to work that friendly display for all it was worth, and she had the tips to prove it.

The attire of Florine, the second bartender, would probably startle even veteran Walmart fashion aficionados, and she too enjoyed generous tips.

Today the five-foot-four Florine, who easily weighed in at a solid 350, wore skin-tight black latex pedal-pushers, black socks and short biker boots, with a loose fitting T-shirt, a washed out print on a white background. Over that she had unwisely layered a way too small black vest, modified with a homemade extender, allowing it to snugly fasten under a generous bosom.

Florine's wrists and biceps were ringed with metal studded black leather bands, and she wore fingerless black leather motorcycle gloves to tend bar. Aviator sunglasses, and a black sports car cap worn over shoulder-length greasy mouse-brown hair, completed today's fashion statement.

Along with a great sense of humor, Florine was perfectly comfortable in her own skin. She was well liked, and generally had two or three boyfriends at any given time.

Sarah grinned and waved to the pair.

While the weekend biker lawyer who was her date this afternoon reviewed his friend's real estate contract, Sarah glanced at the crowd bellied up to the bar. Recognizing a quartet of grizzled bikers, she called them out by name, and crossed the room to give each a hug.

"Anybody seen Big Lou?" she asked Spade, who shrugged before taking a swig of his beer.

"Saw him a few minutes ago." Jack frowned and glanced around.

"He's around here somewhere…" muttered Que. "Yo, Karen," he hailed the bartender, holding an empty beer in the air to get her attention. "Hit me again."

"He's doing business in the corner," Rimp volunteered, nodding in the direction of a table toward the far end of the room.

"Thanks hon," she smiled, then turned and headed toward Big Lou's table. Never a man to miss the approach of a drop-dead gorgeous blonde, Lou glanced up, caught Sarah's eye, and smiled as she headed in his direction.

"Hey sweet thing! Give Big Lou some lovin'," he cheerfully commanded, rising from one of the table's sturdy half-round wooden chairs to give her a hug and affectionately buss her cheek.

"Are you raisin hell again?" Sarah teased.

"Nah, but I'll bet you are," he countered with a wink and sat back down in his chair.

Then, with a concerned look, he gently pulled her onto his lap and spoke in a discrete undertone, so as not to be overheard by his tablemates amidst the din.

"Are you drunk again, sugar?" he asked her, only half-kidding.

Sarah reached over, grabbed the handle of his beer mug and helped herself to a sip.

"Cheers!" she toasted him.

"Why do you look so serious all of a sudden, Big Lou." She gave him a mock frown. "So… am I invited to your club party next month? I plan to dance on the bar again. I might even strip," she laughed.

Lou grinned good naturedly. He reclaimed his beer and took a healthy sip before setting the heavy glass mug back down on the table.

"When's the last time you talked to your family, Sarah?" he asked, looking her dead in the eye.

With mock exasperation she asked, "*Must* you be such a buzz kill, Lou?"

Big Lou smiled, but he was serious.

He was an interesting man, Sarah reflected. Nobody seemed to know for certain what his background was, but it went without saying that he could handle himself in any kind of situation. Nobody needed a demonstration. It was simply one of those things that you just knew in your gut.

Sarah guessed him to be on the near side of fifty. He stood about six-foot-two with a nice build, so he obviously kept himself in shape. Skin tone medium, he looked as if he had a light tan without actually needing one. Maybe some Italian ancestry, Sarah theorized. Lou's dark, close-cropped hair was slightly receding, and he sported a five o'clock shadow. His hazel eyes were friendly but calculating, constantly alert. If she had to guess, Sarah would say former military, probably an elite group, Navy Seals or Delta Force. On the other hand, she thought, you could just as easily have pictured him wearing a five-thousand-dollar bespoke suit, owning a chauffeured limo, and quietly masterminding a major corporate takeover.

Were another man to take Big Lou's measure, what he'd likely see would be a man so secure in himself that he had nothing left to prove, and no one worthy of proving it to.

But for some reason, Lou seemed to genuinely care about Sarah's well-being.

Sarah shrugged and answered his question, "My family's weird, Lou. We're not close. Never have been. I've already told you that. Mostly we don't even know what to say to each other when we do talk."

She paused and grew thoughtful, unconsciously opening a small window to her past with an admission he hadn't heard before.

"It's been that way for as long as I can remember, Lou. Even when I was a little kid. I remember my mother telling me that I was adopted, and my sister was always ragging me, saying that I wasn't a real member of their family.

"But why would somebody go to all the trouble to adopt a kid, hell… I was an infant when they brought me home, for God's sake, and then treat them like shit? I just… don't get it. I have no idea what I did to make them hate me as much as they seem to.

"You know…" she continued. "I never get a call from them on a holiday, they never wish me happy birthday. Actually, to the best of my recollection I've never even had a birthday party. And these days, if I call them, either they recognize the number and don't bother to answer, or if they do answer, there's an argument.

"Christ. I probably should have been named Cinderella instead of Sarah," she laughed bitterly. "This is not healthy; you know what I mean Lou?" She sighed heavily.

"You're a grown woman, Sarah. Why do you still care about that?" Lou asked perceptively. "Can't you put it behind you and move forward with your life?"

"It's still *in* my life, Lou. I'm still getting crap from them, and I still don't understand it. I keep trying to get their attention, keep trying to please them. Maybe that's the problem. Maybe I can't move forward until I do understand it, but... I don't even know how to begin to do that."

"If you did have the answer, do you think you could move forward?" he asked her.

"I'd sure as hell try," she replied. "This situation is *so* not good for my head, Lou.

"Why?" she demanded with a laugh. "Have you got it? Because if you ever figure it out, I'd for damn sure like to hear the answer!" she smiled.

Lou gave her a squeeze. "I'll remind you of that when I figure it out," he joked.

"Think anyone will ever want me to be a part of their life, damaged and all?" she posed the question to Lou quietly, almost as an afterthought.

Without waiting for an answer, she quickly shook herself out of that somber mood. Glancing across the room she saw her date raise his hand to let her know he was ready to go.

Like someone had suddenly flipped a switch, she became chipper again.

Sarah gave him a big smack on the cheek. "Hey, tonight I am dancing and gettin' loaded!" she announced.

"You working in the morning?" he asked.

"Yes sir! Bright and early!" she confirmed. "OK darlin', I'm off."

Smiling and taking a last sip of Lou's beer, she gave him a quick hug, then rose from his lap. To the strains of Aretha Franklin's *Respect,* Sarah danced her way across the floor, waving goodbye to friends as she went. She left the bar on the back of the Harley.

Big Lou watched as she went out the door then solemnly shook his head. *I worry about her,* he thought to himself. Lou raised his mug and drained the rest of the beer, slamming it decisively on the table when he finished.

He nodded and gave a wave in response to a new arrival, a buddy who hailed him from across the room, and headed in his direction.

***

Morning, Sarah sighed. *Thank God for gas stations with coffee,* she thought to herself, as she took a sip from her 24oz cup.

She was comfortably dressed in a pair of GAP™ jeans and a stylish lavender pullover with three-quarter length sleeves. She had added a silk scarf in an abstract design of secondary colors, along with clover colored hoop earrings and a lavender pair of lace-up Skechers™. Her looks and her presentation conveyed the impression that she had her shit together.

To a certain extent that was true.

She came from a well-educated family, both her parents as well as her sister were professionals. Her mother, Pauline Watson, was one of the curators at the

Cleveland Museum of Natural History. Her father, James Watson, a successful certified public accountant, owned a well-respected, medium sized CPA firm. Sarah also had one sister, two years younger, a nurse, with a BSN.

Sarah herself had earned her bachelors in English from Ohio State University, and her Masters in game strategy and decision making, as well as her doctorate of fine arts in creative writing from Ohio University.

After completing her degrees, she had relocated from Ohio to North Carolina. At present, she was teaching technology in the arts, which North Carolina State University in Raleigh dryly defined in their catalog as 'The interaction between technology and the arts with an emphasis on developments in Western art of the twentieth-century. Historical and emerging issues include sound and film recordings, the addition of sound to films, the impact of films and television on theater, the impact of radio, computer applications to music, the visual arts, and literature.'

She actually loved what she was doing. When it came to teaching, anyway.

Sarah stood in front of her class of thirty students, having just completed delivering today's lecture.

"Remember, your outlines are due tomorrow. If you have any questions, either see me during office hours, or shoot me an e-mail. Have a great rest of the day, and I'll see you Wednesday."

She gathered her papers and headed out the door, accidentally overhearing two of her students who were walking slightly ahead of her.

"She is really good. A different kind of teacher, even her style is different. It feels like she not only relates but that she cares. She's so energetic in her lectures, it really keeps you involved in what she's saying." The student laughed. "I'll bet you she's wild when she's away from campus!" he joked.

"I know what you're saying," the second student concurred.

Sarah smiled to herself. *Nice to know that somebody appreciates me,* she thought.

***

Sarah was driving with a printout of a newspaper ad, looking for an address. Three years ago, she had rented a room sight unseen from a friend in Raleigh for a flat monthly amount which included her share of utilities. The friend had assured her it was a real bargain, so she had trustingly signed a long-term lease for the room, only to later learn that the so-called 'friend' had been totally ripping her off. And then, of course, the 'friend' refused to let her out of the lease, which, hallelujah! Was *finally* ending.

"Well," she decided, speaking aloud to herself as she drove. "I will look upon this as a valuable learning experience." Then punctuated the 'learning experience' part with a loudly muttered snarl, "Fucking *bitch!*"

Sarah threw her cigarette out the window. It tasted like dirt anyway. It was probably just the aggravation that had prompted her to light one from that ancient and very stale pack she'd found in the glove compartment. She had stopped smoking cold turkey when she first moved to Raleigh. "Don't need to start that crap up again," she told herself.

Today she was looking at what had been advertised as a 'mother-in-law' apartment for rent in Apex, North Carolina, a town located about twenty minutes from Raleigh. *Pretty place,* she thought, as she drove through it. Quaint. Well maintained. Also very safe, she had read when she researched the area.

Where the hell is this place? She sighed in frustration, shoved her shades up on top of her head, turned down the radio volume and frowned. *OK,* she thought as she glanced at her scribbled notes. Wood fence posts, barbed wire, long dirt road, grass strip between the ruts, and no trespassing signs at the edge of the road. *This must be it.* There was a fairly good-sized two-story home and a little bit further down the same long driveway she could see a small, neatly maintained one-story frame cottage. She pulled in front of the bigger house on the property and parked.

She climbed the front steps to the porch, knocked on the front door and sighed. *Can't believe I'm actually in this kind of financial position at this point in my life. I make* good money. *What the hell is the matter with me? Gotta get my act together.*

She glanced around her as she waited for someone to answer the door. *I could use a drink,* she thought.

The front door suddenly opened. Sarah did a double take and very nearly laughed out loud. The man standing there was probably in his late 60s, his hair was standing straight up, he had a cigarette in one hand, a drink in the other, *and I kid you not,* she thought to herself. *This guy could have been Jack Nicholson's twin brother.*

"Mr. Samuels?" she asked.

"Name's Ed. Are you Sarah?" he inquired with a crooked grin, which made him look even more like his doppelgänger.

"Yes sir," she replied, grinning back at him.

"Where you from?

"Ohio, sir."

Ed laughed out loud. "Huh. I dated a good ole girl from Ohio. Name was Darlene. Dated her for sixteen years. Damn Yankee. Oh, shit, man do I remember Darlene," he intoned fondly.

"May I see the mother-in-law apartment please?"

"Sure! It's open. Go look around and come back after you're through. It's the 5th wheel around back," he said, then abruptly shut the door in her face.

She blinked. *Huh?*

"*Ummm... Okey Dokey,*" she said to herself, then headed back down the front stairs and around the corner to go find the 5th wheel camper, delaying the grand reveal just long enough to trip over a stray piece of firewood. *Shit.* A redneck in an ancient pickup truck drove by, slowing to take a better look at her. Handyman, maybe. She sighed audibly. Place is filled with weirdos. Then she caught sight of the camper. *Oh, my gawd. That's no mother-in-law apartment. Old Ed there has lost his cotton-pickin' mind. No… wait, I'm not going to make a snap judgment, I'm going to keep an open mind about this. I'm going to look inside. And then I'll leave.*

Sarah went up the steps, turned the handle, pulled open the windowed door and glanced inside. *Oh, right. Lovely place. If you don't mind dead bugs.* With a heavy sigh she carefully stepped over the dead roach in the doorway and went inside to look around, leaving the door open.

The camper was furnished in typical mobile home style with ¾ scale furniture. Sofa, couple of armchairs, end table, lamp, and vinyl flooring. Everything looked to be in good shape. Hey, at least there's no shag carpeting. The light switch next to the front door wasn't working. *Maybe the power's off. Good thing it's daylight.* Typical faux pine paneled interior.

Cute little kitchenette, decent amount of cabinet and counter space, double porcelain sink in front of a wide window. Good layout. Built-in ten cubic foot refrigerator/freezer. Whoa, that's a size you don't see every day in a camper. Compact stainless steel drop-in four-burner propane range with oven, and an exhaust fan mounted beneath the overhead cabinets. *Beats the hell out of a hotplate. Yeah, I could make do with that.* Built-in upholstered dinette that seats four. Levolor ™ type blinds on all of the windows, *ooh now there's something cute, the bathroom has a built-in fiberglass shower/tub unit. The tub part is half-size but you could still sort of lean back in a bubble bath and read a good book. I like that. So let's see, bathroom vanity, porcelain sink, mirrored medicine cabinet. Linen closet... Great! It's full of clean sheets, pillowcases, towels and washcloths. That's certainly helpful. Camper style toilet, hmmm, no way this thing still uses a holding tank. The camper must be at least thirty-five or forty years old and it's a safe bet it hasn't moved in years. Five bucks says he's got it hooked up to a septic tank. Let's see... Fresh water supply has to be coming from a well a good distance away, and probably also serves the main house along with the little frame cottage down the road.*

There was a sort of bedroom. Actually, it was a wall-to-wall queen-sized mattress in the elevated forward neck of the camper, the part that would overhang the bed of a pickup truck when it was being towed. The mattress was clean and looked like a fairly recent purchase, so that was a good sign. There was a wall mounted light fixture in the bedroom, and a two-foot square four-inch-tall pedestal nightstand next to a four-plug electric outlet in the corner. The sawed-off nightstand even had a pull-out drawer, so the original wooden legs had either been unscrewed or literally sawn off. It was a clever idea and provided a perfectly workable surface for a clock radio, phone charger, mini-TV, and a reading lamp.

She returned to take a closer look at the living room. *Ewww, dead bug.* She shivered. *Ick. More dead bugs. Whooooo, damn. That sucker's not dead.* She grabbed an old phone book from the counter and flattened him. *Eww. Eww. Eww.*

With a mildly horrified look on her face, Sarah continued the tour.

What am I doing here? I'm a grown-up. I'm a teacher, for Pete's sake. I'm not saddled with kids, thank God. But living in a freaking forty-year-old camper? How big is this thing? It's, let's see, can't be any bigger than 8.5' wide by maybe... twenty-eight feet long, so that's... oh for Pete's sake, that's just ridiculous... How did I even get in this position? My series of bad decisions, I suppose.

Weather's gonna get cold pretty soon. I don't see a source of heat in this thing. Oh wait... what's that? In the corner of the living room next to a small sliding window was a discretely designed, compact 10,000 BTU portable air conditioner with a heating function. She walked over to take a closer look. The instruction manual and remote control sat on top of the unit. *That'll work.*

Oh hell, she thought and headed out the door, slamming it shut behind her.

Bunnnk! The latch failed to function, and the door popped back open. *Crap.* She slammed it shut it a second time and this time it held. P.O.S. camper, Sarah mumbled to herself and sighed heavily.

She went back around the house to the front door and knocked again.

Ed opened the door then turned to head back to wherever the hell he was going and called over his shoulder, "Come on in, girl. So, what did you think?"

Sarah rolled her eyes.

"I'll take it," she replied.

"Seriously?"

"Yeah," she said morosely. "Seriously. But first, talk to me about the electricity and the propane and the bugs. And the toilet. Tell me about the damn toilet."

Ed laughed with delight.

"Great! OK, let me take your questions in order. Electricity: It's cheap but I include it in your rent anyway. Propane for your stove: I got a guy who comes out and tops off the tanks once a month. Also included in your rent. So's internet and cable TV. Toilet and wastewater drains are hooked up to a separate septic system. Don't tell anybody. Building department gets pissed if you do that stuff without a permit.

"Kitchen and bath both have tankless water heaters. Kitchenette's fully equipped as you probably noticed. Coffeemaker, toaster, microwave/convection oven combo. You've got pots, pans, bowls, dishes, glasses, utensils, and a handheld mixer. Garbage pickup is Thursdays. On the far side of the camper there's a shed on a concrete slab. Inside is a washer and dryer. Cold water wash only, I'm afraid. The machines are old but they both still work fine.

The laundry water drains into the flower bed. The azaleas seem to like it."

"Did I forget anything?"

Sarah nodded. "Bugs."

"Right. I got bug bombs. I've also got a spare Shop Vac you can use."

"I'll vacuum up the bugs, but I can't empty a Shop Vac full of dead bugs, Ed. I… just… can't."

Ed burst out laughing. "I'll empty the dead bugs."

"Also, it's quiet out here," he said. "Ain't nobody gonna bother ya. I watch out for who's comin' and goin'. Neighbor down the road's got a dog that raises particular hell if he sees somebody who doesn't belong."

"I didn't see him when I drove in. He didn't bark at me."

"He's a good judge of character. I own some businesses so the road into the compound here sometimes gets a little busy during the day. I'll flip the switches to turn on the utilities for the camper. You can take the keys and I'll give you two weeks free rent. Move in tonight if you like. Your neighbor in the little cracker house is a real nice girl. Rent's due first of the month."

"You need a security deposit?"

Ed looked at her and made a snap decision. "Nah."

"Thanks, Ed." She meant it.

"Take your time, girl. And oh yeah, let me get those bug bombs for ya."

"Where's the closest grocery store, Ed?"

"Next town over. Cary. About ten minutes from here. They've got Walmart, Sam's Club, Publix, Starbucks, that kind of stuff. It's a regular place. There's a direction sign points to Cary at the end of the driveway. Whatever you need, if it's not in Apex you'll definitely find it in Cary. Tell you what... If you're heading into Cary to do some shopping, I'll set off the bug bombs and have the dead bugs vacuumed up before you get back."

"Deal!" Sarah said. "Need anything from the store?"

"Grab a carton of orange juice. Once you get settled, we'll have screwdrivers out by the fire pit in the backyard."

Sarah gave him a genuine smile. "Works for me."

Yeah, she said to herself. *Actually it does.*

Sarah took her time to allow Ed to conduct the bug bomb and bug removal drill. First, she drove around Apex, and then she drove around Cary to familiarize herself with the lay of the land, before hitting the grocery store.

By the time she got back to the 5th wheel she was pleased to see that Ed had been as good as his word. One last bug staggered into the middle of the camper floor and fell over dead, feet in the air.

"Drama queen," she said sarcastically, then grabbed a tissue to pick up the body and flush him down the toilet.

Sarah unloaded her groceries, paper goods and cleaning supplies and put them away, filled the two plastic ice cube trays with water and stuck them in the freezer, then started unloading the car and bringing in her modest stash of possessions. Clothes, shoes, laptop, printer, diplomas, clock radio, that kind of stuff. Once she had everything put away, she grabbed the carton of orange juice from the refrigerator and knocked on Ed's door.

"Mind if I take a rain check on the screwdriver?" She apologized as she handed him the carton. "I teach at the university, and I just realized that I've still got to get my class work together for tomorrow."

"No problem," he assured her. "And deduct the orange juice from the rent."

She shook her head no. "My treat," she told him with a grin.

Sarah walked back to the 5th wheel and looked around again once she was inside. *Jeez, this place is small. It's the size of a freaking clothes closet. Whatever possessed me to move into this thing?*

She answered her own question. Because it was cheap, and safe, and within commuting distance. And because my landlord's a hoot. She shrugged. *What the hell. I'm already here. I can do this.*

Sarah poured herself a stiff rum and coke, finished unpacking, got her schoolwork together, then poured herself a second stiff rum and coke. On an empty stomach. Somewhere in the back of her head a little voice mentioned that she was probably going to regret not having something to eat.

***

The volume knob on Sarah's old clock radio had obviously been bumped at some point during the move, because when six a.m. rolled around and the alarm clicked on, the day's weather report nearly blew her out of bed.

"Holy *shit!*" she yelped, heart pounding, eyes open wide. She quickly rolled over and slammed her palm on top of the radio several times, searching for the elusive off button.

Finally achieving her goal, she collapsed back against the pillow while she groaned and caught her breath.

Well, there's the morning's cardiac stress test, she thought wearily.

"Morning. Shit. Here we go again. Get *up* Sarah!" she told herself as she rolled out of bed and staggered into the tiny bathroom.

Glancing at her image in the mirror over the postage-stamp sized sink, she winced. Her hair looked like it had been through a hurricane. The rest of her didn't look all that hot either. She groaned again. *Get it together girl, you're going to be facing rush-hour traffic today. Coffee. I need coffee. Also, aspirin. I definitely need aspirin. Should've had dinner.*

A couple of weeks later, Sarah had gone jogging along the Haddon Hall Greenway, a 1.6 mile lightly trafficked loop, part of a trail which ran along the lakefront of Haddon Hall, a luxury home community in Apex.

Cold and sweaty, she had begun to shiver on the drive home and found herself longing for a hot shower. She pulled the car up next to the 5th wheel and headed for the door. It felt unseasonably cold inside the camper. The weather had taken a sudden turn and the temperature was dropping like a stone. She flipped the light switch on and nothing happened. Tried a few more switches and got the same result. *Oh hell. Now what?* She grabbed her phone and dialed Ed.

"Hey girl! What's up?"

"Ed I just got home. I have no power and it's fucking freezing."

"Hang on. I'll be there in a minute."

Click.

Sarah blinked, then yelled at the deadline on her phone. "Asshole!"

Who just hangs up? I really don't feel very good, I'm freezing cold, and I feel like I'm coming down with something. I feel like I'm losing my damn mind.

Common sense kicked in and Sarah put a large pot of water on to boil. Thank God for propane stoves. The heat and the steam would quickly take the edge off the cold. She even also used some of the hot water to make instant cocoa, she reasoned. And if push came to shove and the power was truly out, she could also put on a second pot, warm some water for a shallow tub bath or if necessary, a sponge bath.

The fact that she could actually deal with this was cold comfort to Sarah. That she truly didn't feel well merely added to her annoyance with the unplanned inconvenience.

There was a knock on the door.

"You in there, girl?" Ed called out.

Sarah opened the door to find Ed standing on the steps. He had a cigarette in his mouth, and he was holding two disposable double-walled hot mugs, one of which he handed to Sarah.

"Hot toddy. Bourbon, honey, lemon juice, and hot water. It'll warm you right up."

She gratefully took a sip and sighed. "Oh, God that's good. Thank you!"

"Come on in, Ed. What happened?"

He shook his head no thanks and remained on the steps. "I'm not sure. Something popped the breaker for this specific circuit. I tried resetting it, but nothing happened. I've already called the electrician. He promised he'd be out here as soon as possible. I'm going to go back to the electrical panel and try something else.

"I see you've already done the logical stuff," he commented, nodding toward the now steaming pot of water on the stove. "You're welcome to use the guest room in the main house, Sarah. It's got its own bathroom."

"Thanks, Ed, but I'll wing it until the electrician shows up. In the meantime, I'm starting to really feel like shit. It kinda' feels like strep throat. So, I'm just going to clean up and crawl into bed."

Ed nodded. "Good plan. You got any antibiotics on hand? I have some if you don't."

Sarah nodded. "I'm a teacher. As a breed we pretty much stay prepared. I've still got a nearly full bottle of amoxicillin in the medicine cabinet, and I took a pill the minute I walked in the door," she told him.

"Good girl. All right, make sure you turn off the top burners before you go to bed. Turn the oven on, leave the oven door closed, and set it at 250. That will keep the temperature comfortable inside the camper. Do you have a storm kit? A battery-operated cell phone charger? A bunch of AA batteries? If not, I'll bring supplies out to you. I don't want you in the camper alone without any way to contact me if you need help."

"I've got a storm kit in the linen closet, Ed. Got a couple of chargers and a living ton of batteries in there with them. And I've got a bunch of battery-operated LED lights that could keep the place lit up like a Christmas tree, so I'm in pretty good shape. But that's a good idea, Ed, thanks for reminding me."

"Would you like me to bring you another hot toddy, or do you have the fixings in the camper? How about chicken soup, do you have any chicken soup?"

Sarah couldn't help but laugh. "Florence Nightingale," she teased. "I've got all the basics in house, but I sure do, thank you, Ed."

"OK," he suggested. "Leave one light switch on so you'll know when the power comes back up."

"Will do."

"Lock the door after me."

Sarah laughed again. "Yes, Daddy," she teased him.

"Feel better!" he said, then gave the temperamental camper door a decent slam to make sure it closed. He waited to hear Sarah lock it before he turned and headed back to the house.

Sarah put a second large pot of water on to boil, turned the oven on and set it to 250, then went into the bathroom to prepare a shallow bath. She inserted the drain plug, drew about an inch of cold water, tossed a washcloth in the tub then went to retrieve the pots of hot water. The combination gave her a bath in the tiny tub that was just comfortably past lukewarm, which definitely did the job.

Once she was clean and dry, Sarah pulled on a pair of flannel PJ's and a heavy pair of gym socks, then heated a bowl of chicken soup and made herself another hot toddy. All of her muscles ached. She must be catching something.

"I don't have time for this," she whimpered to herself.

Sarah then hooked up one of emergency chargers and topped off her cell phone's battery. Ed's property had excellent internet reception so she could use her phone to watch TV or listen to music, neither of which she felt like doing at the moment.

Common sense said there was no way she was going to suddenly feel wonderful in the morning, so she emailed both the school and her student list, told them she was calling in sick and that class was cancelled for the rest of the week.

Sarah felt like shit. She finally crawled into bed and allowed herself the luxury of a good cry.

"I can't do this. I don't belong here. Hell, I don't belong anywhere. Nothing ever makes sense," she sobbed, and finally, emotionally exhausted, she cried herself to sleep.

Chapter Two

Sense of Humor (Trying To)

Sarah had forgotten to kill the alarm for the following morning, so bright and early the bloody thing went off again, blasting the day's weather report.

    She could barely move, and her throat felt like she was swallowing nails. It was a Herculean effort just to reach over and smack the off button. That done, she grabbed the bottled water and pills which sat on the little nightstand, took another antibiotic, then rolled over and went back to sleep. That drill would pretty much set the tone for the next several days.

    Ed's buddy the electrician had shown up within an hour and temporarily bootlegged shore power to the camper. He'd then made an appointment to come back later in the week to do a major upgrade to the electrical panel.

    Ed called the camper mid-morning on the second day to check up on her. "How are you feeling?"

    "I feel like shit," she groaned.

    "You need anything?" he asked.

    "I need a life."

"I'll make a note of that," he quipped. "I left a bag on your steps. Matzo ball soup, orange juice, a tub of pudding and a carton of ice cream. I hope you like chocolate."

His announcement was met with a moment of stunned silence.

"How on earth did you find matzo ball soup in Apex?" she finally asked.

"There are a bunch of really good delicatessens in Cary," he replied.

"If I didn't feel so totally crappy, I'd run over and give you a hug."

"Grab the bag from the steps then go back to bed," he advised. "You can give me a rain check on the hug."

"Deal," she said.

"Feel better," he told her and then simply hung up.

"Asshole," she laughed, somewhat painfully. "The guy never remembers to say goodbye."

Sarah dragged herself out of bed to retrieve the bag from the steps. She poured herself a glass of orange juice, then put the cold stuff away in the little refrigerator/freezer. There were two large plastic tubs in a smaller insulated bag, one full of matzo balls, the other filled with chicken soup. She put some of both in a bowl and heated it in the microwave. *Heavenly,* she thought, as she tasted it. Then she crawled back into bed.

For the next few days, she periodically roused herself for long enough to stagger to the bathroom or wander out to the kitchen for either a bowl of soup or a cup of ice cream or chilled pudding to sooth her aching throat.

She eventually felt like she might actually live, so she'd thrown on a pair of jeans and a light sweater and was sitting at the little dinette table in the camper, working on her laptop, reviewing student papers, when there was a knock at the door.

"Who is it?" she called.

"Ed."

She smiled then rose and opened the door. "Hello."

He had a very tall, insulated coffee mug with a top on it in each hand and the ever-present cigarette in his mouth. He held one of the covered mugs up and nodded toward it to indicate that one was for her.

"Feeling better?" he inquired.

"Thank you," she said as she looked at the mug with interest. "I'm not a hundred percent yet, but I'm certainly a lot better, thanks."

"I thought this might cheer you up some," he said.

"What is it?"

"Irish coffee. With freshly whipped cream."

"Oooooooh…" she sighed with longing.

"You need some fresh air. Throw on a sweater, come on out and sit by the fire pit with me. I'll carry your drink for you."

"Give me thirty seconds," she said and pulled the door shut. She struggled into an oversized university sweatshirt, pulled a bright red wool snood over her head, loosely wrapping the long scarf ends around her neck and shoulders, slipped her sock-covered feet into a pair of short leather boots and jammed a pair of cashmere gloves into the back pocket of her jeans. She was literally dressed and out the door in twenty-eight seconds.

Ed grinned. "You are talented beyond your years," he laughed with delight. "You remind me of Little Red Riding Hood in that thing."

She grinned right back at him.

***

Ed, comfortably bundled in his Members Only jacket and a ski cap, occupied one of the six roomy plastic chairs grouped around the friendly fire pit in his backyard. Sara had chosen to perch atop the adjacent white lacquered A-frame picnic table, her boots resting on the bench seat. She cradled the steaming cup of Irish coffee between her gloved hands, and happily licked a mustache-sized smootch of whipped cream from her upper lip.

"You know you're spoiling me, right?" she asked, with a raised eyebrow.

Ed shrugged. "I feed stray cats. I look in on sick tenants. No big thing," he brushed off his thoughtfulness.

Sarah casually glanced around her. Open space. Trees. Peace and Quiet. A giant pile of firewood, the scent of pine, a roaring fire with warmth she could feel from where she sat.

She enjoyed the companionable silence.

"Where 'bouts in Ohio you from, Sarah?" Ed asked conversationally.

"Central," she replied noncommittally.

"Brothers or sisters?" he asked.

Startled, she looked at him, momentarily taken aback at having been hit with a personal question.

"One sister. Couple of years younger. She's a nurse. She's also a vicious bitch."

Sarah actually surprised herself by being so forthright.

"What do your mom and dad do?"

"She's a curator with the Natural History Museum, he's a CPA."

"You guys all get along well?"

"Nope," she said flatly. Subject closed.

Sarah decided to turn the tables and ask some questions of her own.

"Who lives in that little cracker house back there? It's yours, right?"

He nodded. "It's mine. A lady lives there. Just landed a real good job 'bout eighty miles west of here, over in High Point. She'll be moving out next month."

"It's bigger than the camper, right?"

"Yep."

"Can I move in?"

"Rent's higher."

"OK," she agreed, and just like that, the matter was settled.

Slightly less than a month later the little 'cracker house' was empty. As in, it was unfurnished. OK, there was a couch, but beyond that, it was empty. She'd eventually have to hunt for some used furniture. She figured she'd start moving a bit at a time while still camping in the 5th wheel.

Happily, the tenant had left it clean as a whistle, so once again Sarah was in the process of packing and moving. Sarah seriously hated the moving process. She considered it a pain in the ass. She was also on her fourth rum and coke, which might have influenced her opinion. The tall tumblers contained mostly rum, and they were a little light on the Coca-Cola™ part of the rum and coke cocktail.

She was kneeling on the floor in the kitchen and had just finished filling the second of two good-sized boxes containing the contents of her erstwhile liquor cabinet. Sarah paused and looked at all the bottles. She frowned as a thought occurred to her amidst a sudden wave of dizziness.

It's possible I may be drinking a tad too much.

She sighed, rose to her feet then lifted the box and set it on the dinette table. Glancing around she spied her framed MA diploma laying on one of the bench seats of the dinette. Grabbing it, she balanced it on top of the bottles, hoisted the heavy box and headed for the camper door. She had successfully made it down the steps but when she turned to nudge the door shut with the swing of a hip she lost her balance, the bottles shifted, and she collapsed in a heap on the ground in front of the Civic.

"*Shit!*" she yelped as she fell, and near two dozen bottles spilled out of the box and rolled onto the dirt driveway. She rolled over on her back and lay there, the framed MA certificate somehow safely clutched in one hand.

"Goddamn it to hell," she said to herself as she gazed skyward.

"Ouch!" She frowned, as she mentally took stock of her condition and realized that she'd landed a little heavily on one hip. "*That's* gonna leave a mark."

She rolled over, propped herself up on her elbows and looked around as she lay there. Bottles were scattered everywhere but nothing had broken. The box was ripped, though. She'd need another one. And of course, her hair and clothes and arms were now filthy dirty from lying in the dirt.

"Son of a bitch," she sighed. "Story of my life."

Sarah pushed herself over and up until she had reached a casual sitting position. Then, wrapping her arms around her knees she wearily rested her head on her forearms and knees.

Ed had been sitting at a desk by the window and heard Sarah cry out as she lost her balance. He had sprung to his feet, intending to rush out and help, but paused when he realized she hadn't been hurt.

He'd continued to stand next to his desk and he watched with interest, observing the way she was handling the situation. She had lain there for a moment, gazing skyward as she mentally assessed her physical condition, then propped herself up on her elbows to evaluate the condition of the articles she had been carrying. She had instinctively protected something she considered important during the fall, which from here looked to be a framed diploma. Then she had sat up and rested her head on her knees, taking stock of her mental situation.

Ed wasn't a psychologist, but he had a pretty good grasp of the human condition. She had probably been drinking. Were Sarah to realize that her fall had been seen, she'd be embarrassed, angry with herself, and possibly even defensive.

Clearly, she wasn't physically injured, and by the looks of her, she appeared to be emotionally struggling with something far more painful than the fall.

He decided to leave her be.

Holy shit, Ed thought to himself with a sigh. *I've gotta help this girl.*

He walked over to the bar in his study, grabbed a crystal tumbler and poured himself a light splash of scotch before returning to his desk to sit back down. Ed shook his head, lit a cigarette, and leaned back in his chair, a faraway look in his eyes.

"Goddamn Yankees," he said with a smile.

***

As Sarah sat there in the dirt, head on her knees, she had flashed back to a childhood memory.

It had been a Thanksgiving holiday. Her mother, Pauline was making the turkey, and both of Sarah's grandmothers had been invited to join them for dinner. At the conclusion of dinner, the adults adjourned to the living room for coffee and Sarah was instructed to clear the table. One by one she carried the good china plates to the kitchen, scraped, rinsed and carefully stacked them on the counter next to the sink. Serving bowls containing leftovers were to be placed on the kitchen's breakfast table for Pauline to deal with later.

The last thing sitting on the lace tablecloth which covered the dining room table was a small but valuable old vase that had been in Jim's family for a number of generations. Pauline usually kept it inside the big Cherry breakfront, but she'd fill it with flowers and use it as a centerpiece on special occasions like holidays.

Sarah was only seven, but she knew to be extra careful. She had done this before. She would carry it into the kitchen and carefully set it on the breakfast table. Pauline could then transfer the flowers to a casual vase before gently washing and drying the antique vase, pursuant to returning it to the glassed-in breakfront.

Sarah had firmly grasped the little vase with both hands and was walking slowly, headed down the hall to the kitchen. Her spoiled and spiteful five-year-old sister, Jackie had snuck up behind her and deliberately lodged a vicious kick at the back of Sarah's right knee. Sarah had screamed in pain when the hard-soled patent leather Mary Jane shoe struck the back of her knee, rupturing a small vein in her leg in the process. Her leg had buckled, pitching her forward, and the valuable old vase had gone flying, jettisoned from her hands onto the cold porcelain tile floor, shattering into a thousand pieces.

Five-year-old Jackie had launched the sneak attack on her sister, then turned and sprinted stealthily back into her own bedroom to establish her alibi. She had kicked off her Mary Janes, thrown herself on the floor, and pretended to have been playing with her dolls.

Naturally everyone came running at the sound of the scream and the crash. Everyone but Jackie, who finally padded out of her bedroom, wearing her lace-edged white socks, timing her arrival on the scene about a minute after everyone else had shown up.

"What happened, Mommy?" little Jackie had asked her mother, feigning wide-eyed innocence as she looked at the debris field. "Oh *no!* Did Sarah break your special vase?"

Sarah was gasping with pain and shock. She was literally covered with streaks of blood, having landed on the sharp porcelain shards.

There was much screaming and gnashing of teeth, and when Sarah had struggled to her feet, she tried to explain that Jackie had run up behind her and kicked her with her hard Mary Janes.

Pauline had flown into a full-blown rage, screaming at the top of her lungs, *"She's not even wearing shoes, you useless fucking piece of shit spawn of a whore bastard liar!"* And she slapped Sarah so hard the blow had literally knocked her halfway across the room. Her father had run over to her, yanked her up by the arm and whaled the living daylights out of her butt, screaming in outrage that nobody had wanted her, and he wished she had never been born.

The grandmothers seemed more concerned with retrieving a broom, dustpan, and vacuum to clean up the mess. Nobody noticed five-year-old Jackie standing off in the corner, smiling spitefully, wearing a superior look on her face.

It took Pauline's black and blue handprint on Sarah's face two solid weeks to fade. She was kept home from school until it disappeared. The child had a noticeable bruise on the back of her right knee. If her parents had noticed the bruise, they apparently chose not to acknowledge it.

Sarah was locked in her room and given only one meal a day, a bowl of cold cereal, for the entire two-week period.

Seven-year-old Sarah had washed the blood off all by herself, applied iodine and band aids to the largest cuts, put her jammies on, then crawled into bed and pulled the covers over her little head.

She dared not allow herself to cry. She didn't want to make anybody mad.

Life had gone downhill from there. Sarah had no memory of ever having been hugged by anyone throughout her entire childhood. But where once her life had only been achingly lonely, from that point on there had been constant insults and accusations and belittling from the three of them.

She could never figure out what it was she must have done to make all of them so angry with her.

Funny how memories like that stick with you, she thought.

I am so tired of trying to be good enough. So tired of being told I'm useless and good for nothing, a worthless screw-up who will never amount to anything. Tired of being told that I'm not even a real member of the family, nobody wanted me and they should have taken me back to the adoption people.

Dammit, I'm not worthless, and I'm sure as hell not stupid. I put myself through school and I earned advanced degrees from two major universities.

Sarah rose, determinedly, if somewhat unsteadily, shook the dirt out of her hair, brushed herself off, grabbed the torn cardboard box and went back inside the camper in search of some reinforced packing tape. Once she had mended the box, she'd retrieve the bottles and finish packing the car for this trip.

***

Same old. Same old. There goes the alarm clock. Sigh... Back to work.

Sarah stood at the podium in her classroom. She had on a pair of her goes-with-everything Gap jeans accented with a yellow silk shell of a blouse, a navy-blue blazer and ankle high brown leather boots. Today she had pulled her hair back in a low ponytail with a sunshine yellow scrunchie and added nickel-sized plain gold button earrings. Granted she was still a little hungover, but she looked good.

"Everybody ready for their presentations today?" she asked, pausing to take a sip of her coffee. A couple of hands went up.

"Not ready? Really? Why not?"

A male student who looked as hungover as Sarah felt, shrugged and said, "I forgot."

A wan looking female sighed. She looked exhausted. "Ma'am, my mom died."

"I'm so sorry for your loss," Sarah said. "Go on home, sweetheart, try to get some rest.

"And as for you, Fred... for fuck's sake man, buy a stack of Post-It™ notes and stick reminders on the damn refrigerator. All right. I'll let the both of you know your make-up dates."

After class Sarah stopped by the dean's office, still feeling the aftereffects of a hangover. She felt like crap, but the dean had asked her to stop by for a minute when she got a chance.

She opened the door and greeted the dean's secretary. "Hello Judy."

Judy's eyes lit up. "Hi Sarah, I'm sorry but you just missed the dean, she had to run out unexpectedly. She probably won't be back for another hour or so."

"No problem. I can come back another time. How was your weekend?"

"It was awesome!"

"Yeah? What'd you do?"

"I went out dancing!" Judy gushed excitedly.

"Nice!" Sarah smiled while mentally doing a slight double take. To say that Judy was a bit zaftig would be a masterpiece of an understatement. The girl was built like a tank. Also, her makeup appeared to have been troweled on. Today she was wearing half-inch long fake eyelashes and royal-blue glitter eye shadow which, although designed to be transparently applied for evening wear, had been solidly painted on, from her eyelids to her heavily penciled eyebrows. She resembled a deranged raccoon.

"Yeah, I saw so many friends there…" Judy continued. "I danced all night long. It was absolutely great!"

"Very cool. Where'd y'all go? Maybe I'll check it out."

"All of us were at Second Life."

"Oh, really? How fun!"

"Yeah, just sign up with Second Life and you can join in the fun anytime!"

Sarah's jaw dropped slightly, then she quickly recovered. "Yeah, will do."

Mentally Sarah connected the dots. Second Life was a Ready Player One style of virtual world. Urban Dictionary described it as, 'A game where desperate people with no lives or friends get to live out their dreams of social acceptance and sex… the vast majority of Second Life players are unattractive and socially awkward.'

Omg. Sarah smiled, glanced at her watch and feigned being late. "Oh golly, I'm running late. I'll catch the dean another time. Take care, Judy, have fun!"

"See you there!" Judy called back.

A tiny whimper escaped Sarah's lips once she was out of earshot. *Virtual sex with an avatar. Jeezus. I saw Ready Player One. Some of those avatars were weirder than shit. Especially that giant lobster-looking thing.*

Well now, let's look at this rationally. It's safe, right? Nobody knows who anybody else really is, so it's perfectly safe. And as long as Judy's having a good time, there's no harm done. So that's all that really counts.

Then she rolled her eyes.

Gawd. I could really use a drink. She headed for the parking lot and decided to go home instead.

Sarah pulled into the compound and parked next to the 5th wheel. She hadn't even gotten out of the car before her phone rang.

"Hey girl, wanna go for a ride?" asked Ed.

"Where we going?"

"Come on over, I'll fix you a drink and we'll go to the post office."

Sarah shrugged. She had no plans, and she was perfectly amenable to having a drink with a friend.

"OK. Let me just drop off my stuff and I'll be right there."

As usual, Ed simply hung up without saying bye.

Ed's door was unlocked so Sarah just walked in and yelled. "I'm here, where are you?"

He yelled back, "Kitchen."

"Hey!" she said cheerfully, then held both hands out. "I have something for you. I brought my own traveling cup," she grinned, handing him a pair of tall, double-walled plastic tumblers, each with its own matching straw. "I bought one for each of us. Green one's mine, blue one's yours. I've already washed them."

"Thank you!" he said, delighted with his new toy. He set the glasses down on the counter. "Here, go ahead and fix us a couple of rum and cokes to go while I grab my jacket, and let's blow this pop stand."

Five minutes later, the two of them were in Ed's new Cadillac Escalade, a fat brown envelope with a ribbon of postage having been tossed in the back seat. They were heading for Raleigh.

"They don't have a post office in Apex?" Sarah asked curiously.

"Sure. But I felt like taking a ride."

"OK." Sarah nodded agreeably.

Ed set his tumbler in the center console cup holder while he lit a cigarette.

They traveled in peaceable silence for a moment then Ed suddenly announced, "It all boils down to one thing, Sarah."

"What's that, Ed?" she asked, taking a sip of her strong rum and coke.

"Money," he stated decidedly. "The American dollar."

Sarah took another sip. "Yep, sure does," she agreed.

"How much debt you got? How much is your car note?" he asked.

"$330 a month."

"Day-yum, girl. Get that muther paid off. There is no greater freedom than being debt-free and owing nobody."

"Will do." Sarah nodded.

"How much credit card debt you got?"

"Too much. About fifteen grand."

"Shee-yit, Sarah. Get it paid."

"Will do."

Ed pulled into the Cary post office driveway, edged up to the drop box, rolled down the window, reached into the back seat to retrieve the brown envelope then shoved it into the mailbox opening. He listened for the satisfying thunk as it hit the bottom of the mailbox then pushed the button to roll the window back up. He pulled out of the parking lot and continued driving toward Raleigh.

Sarah gave a discreet shake of her head but said nothing for a few minutes until curiosity got the better of her.

"Where are we going now?" she asked. Curiously.

"Ghetto."

"Okey Dokey."

Ed reached for his travel cup and took a satisfying sip of his drink.

They stopped for a traffic light.

"Assholes!" he announced, gesturing toward the car in the next lane. "People can't drive. Always on that telephone. You're not supposed to be on the telephone when you drive."

Sarah grinned mischievously. "I think we're also not supposed to drink."

"Your travel cup makes it look like we've got soft drinks," he noted astutely before continuing with his other-driver rant.

"You know how I always look to my left and right when I drive, make sure I know where everybody is. But it's always the same thing. People are either eating or they're texting, instead of paying attention to the road. And they're fat."

Not exactly sure how texting and fat were related, Sarah just took another sip of her drink and agreed with the comment on the grounds of distracted driving.

"I know. It's bullshit. You can get killed that way. They're fucking idiots."

Ed took the next turn which put him in a more modest part of Raleigh. As he drove, he commented to Sarah, "Look at all these people. Rims and nice cars, no jobs, no money."

"Yup. Bullshit. Bull. Shit."

"Be glad you got yourself a job and an education."

"Yessir, I am indeed grateful for that."

Ed had begun chain smoking. "Be glad you don't have any bambinos at this point in your life, you'd never be able to dig your way out of a hole with that kind of responsibility hanging around your neck."

Sarah shook her head. "I don't want kids. Nope. Fuck that. No kids."

Ed took the next turn, looped around and headed back toward the way they had come.

"OK, nice ride," he announced. "Let's go home."

Sarah nodded her agreement, thinking, *Well, that was weird.*

Sarah lay in bed that night, cruising through the web on her iPhone. *I need to get some regular exercise. I should probably join a gym.* She searched for one located near the university and decided to swing by and take a look at it the following day after class.

The address of the gym she had chosen to look at was convenient enough, but it turned out to be a dated 70s era gym. The old guy behind the desk, whom she assumed was the owner, looked overweight and moderately surly, but he had an employee, a young guy who looked pretty fit.

The old guy wore a nametag that said 'Jack.'

"Hi," she said as she stepped up to the desk. "I might be interested in joining." He didn't bother to look up from his computer screen.

"Go ahead and look around," he mumbled.

"Will do," she replied, thinking, *Asshole.* She then wandered around for a bit.

Dead cockroach in the lady's locker room. Ick.

Well at least it's dead, she thought, as she returned to the front desk.

"How much, month-to-month?" she asked Jack, the old guy wearing the nametag.

"Twenty bucks."

"OK, I'll give it a try."

"Yo! Ron, c'mere," he barked, as he reached into a drawer and pulled out a month-to-month membership contract.

"Print yer name and address and contact info on the top lines then sign on the bottom. That'll be twenty bucks." He handed her a membership card with a number that matched the number on the contract. Then he slapped a numbered locker key on the counter. "Don't lose the key," he cautioned. "I don't have a spare."

"Ah, there you are," he said, looking up when the young guy arrived at the desk. "This is Ron, and he's here to help. Ron this is… uh…"

"My name is Sarah," she said, holding out her hand to Ron, who smiled.

"You starting your workout today?" he asked her.

Sarah shook her head. "I'll probably swing by tomorrow around three, I'll start then."

He smiled again. "See you tomorrow," he said, and headed back toward the treadmill.

She looked at the exterior of the building as she left. "What the hell was I thinking?" Sarah asked herself when she got back into her car.

It was around four in the afternoon by the time Sarah pulled into the long driveway from the main road that led into the compound. She was about halfway down the drive before she was able to definitively identify whose Harley it was that was parked in front of the 5th wheel. Once she recognized it, she broke into a big grin. She parked, hopped out of the car and gave Big Lou a bear hug.

"Are you OK? Is everything all right?" she asked him.

"Sure, why?"

"You're here. So, what's up? You sure you're, OK?" she asked as she unlocked the camper door. "Come on in," she invited, and although it was a bit chilly, she left the door wide open. It seemed to make the place feel a little bit bigger.

"How are you sweetheart?" he asked her from his perch on the sofa.

"Never better. When's your club party? I joined a gym today."

He gave her a once over and pronounced her fit. "You don't need it."

"I just figured that I could use the exercise. Employee is hot but owner was a dick."

Lou smiled at the characterization of the staff.

"I was worried about you. I hadn't seen or heard from you in a couple weeks," he said.

"Rum and coke for you?" she offered.

"I'm driving," he reminded her. "I'll take a sip of yours."

"I'm OK, Lou. Really. Just trying to figure out how to get my act together. Turns out this tiny little place is actually not half bad, and my landlord, Ed, is an absolute hoot. He's an older guy, and he keeps an eye on me to make sure I'm OK. I was sick with strep throat at one point, and without saying a word he drove over to a deli in the next town, bought a giant order of matzo ball soup, orange juice, chocolate ice cream and chocolate pudding for me. Even offered me antibiotics if I needed them. But I already had some."

"You know, I actually find that reassuring," Lou said with a smile, and Sarah grinned back.

"I'm OK, Lou. Really. No worries."

"Party's this weekend," he told her. "You coming?" he asked. He held out a hand and she passed him her glass to take a sip.

"Damn that's strong!" He blinked and handed the glass back to her.

"If I'm invited, I'll definitely be there," she told him.

"No drama this weekend, Sarah," he cautioned.

"What's that supposed to mean?" she asked defensively.

"Well, near as I can tell from the grapevine, and I don't know whether this is true or not, but word is, you fucked three of my guys and then made sure their wives knew about it."

Sarah visibly winced.

"You also have a tendency to get tad hostile when you've had too much to drink."

"I do?" Sarah winced again.

"Yes ma'am, you do. Look, I always have your back, sugar, but you have got to slow down."

"So... you're saying that if I got on the stripper pole, I'd probably be giving your girls a run for their money?" she asked jokingly.

"Baby girl, hear me. I love you, but the guys are nervous."

Sarah laughed. "Seriously? Jesus H. Christ. OK, OK! I'll stick to three drinks and then leave. I promise. Don't worry, I won't embarrass you."

"Have you talked to your family lately?" he asked.

"No," she said petulantly and slammed the rest of her drink.

"Why do you keep on asking?" she demanded.

"Honey, you need guidance. You can't hide behind work all of the time. And drinking yourself into a coma is sure as hell not the solution. You worry me, baby girl. I care about you."

With that he rose, kissed her on the top of her head and went out the door. A moment later she heard the engine turn over then the roar of the Harley, as Lou drove away.

Sarah sighed, sat down on the front steps and contemplated the glass of rum and coke in her hand.

"Shit," she muttered, as an errant tear rolled down her cheek.

***

Sarah sighed. She had a headache. Next stop would be her last class for the day. She needed to stop by the university office for a second, conduct her next class, then she could hustle on over to the gym for a quick workout.

Sarah's favorite secretary was all by herself, pouring over one of those comic book-sized local ad mailers. Sarah guessed that Lana probably wore a size twenty. She clearly had no interest in diets, and she good naturedly described herself as having been built for comfort.

When Sarah entered the office, Lana was admiring an ad for a weave.

"Hi Lana..." Sarah didn't have a chance to say anything else. Lana was already on a roll.

"Ooh, look at *this!* Honey, if I wasn't still supportin' my daughter while's she's in school I woulda' had me one of them weaves already. Would you just look at that?" Lana waved the picture of a drop-dead gorgeous black model with roughly a zillion dollar hairdo at Sarah. "Can't you just see me with this?"

Sarah grinned. "Absolutely!"

"What you been up to, girl?... Oooh lookie here..." Lana's attention span had switched gears with the turn of a page. "I can get me a manicure *and* a pedicure for thirty bucks. They's right around the corner. I definitely gotta' check this place out." Lana ripped the page out of the mailer and tossed the rest of the junk mail in the trash.

"Oh listen, before I forget, look here, girl," she said, reaching for a plastic shopping bag under her desk. "I brought you a coupla' pair of pants I found while I was unpackin' some new donations at the Goodwill store. Grabbed 'em up before anybody else had a chance. They's brand new, honey, mmmm-hmmm, they's still got the tags on 'em. From me to you!" Lana pulled just enough material out of the bag so that Sarah could see the colors. Lana quickly stuffed them back in the bag, rose, and slapped the bag on the counter in front of Sarah...

"Thank you, Lana. That was so sweet of you! So, what's new? You're obviously still working your part-time job over at Goodwill?"

Sarah reached into her lightweight leather messenger bag and deposited a binder-clipped sheaf of papers into the in-basket on the counter.

"Yes ma'am," Lana confirmed. "I flat out love that place. You would not believe the stuff people just give away. You let me know if you need anything else from there, you hear? I'll keep an eye open."

"Will do," Sarah said as she glanced at her watch. "Whoops. Gotta' go teach, Ms. Lana, thank you again. Catch you later."

***

Sarah pulled into the parking lot at the gym and while she was retrieving her workout clothes, she took a moment to glance at the slacks Lana had just gifted her with. She promptly burst out laughing.

Sarah wore a size six. The tags on both pair of pants were clearly marked size sixteen.

Bemused, she shook her head, then laughed out loud when she removed them from the bag and held them up. *Ohmygawd. Hip-huggers. These are like... from the 70s. They belong in a freaking museum.*

Ah well, it's the thought that counts, she giggled again. And truly it really was a sweet gesture. *But day-yum these things are dog ugly.*

Sarah quickly stuffed them back into their shopping bag and idly wondered where she could donate them so they wouldn't end up back at Lana's branch of Goodwill. She sighed. *I'll just have to deal with that later.*

She beeped the car locks shut, stuffed the car key in her bag, and headed for the gym.

The old guy was nowhere to be seen and the hunk was sitting at the front desk. He looked up and smiled.

"Hey," she greeted him. "Ron, wasn't it?"

"You came back," he sounded surprised.

"Yeah. Why do you say that?"

"You certainly don't look like you need to lose any weight and your muscles are pretty well toned. You a jogger?"

"I run some when I have the time. Been a little busy lately. I'm gonna go change. Maybe hit the treadmill."

By the time she returned the old guy was back at the front desk, Ron was on one treadmill, and he motioned for her to join him on the adjacent treadmill.

They walked side by side for forty minutes.

"I need to find a trainer," Sarah told him.

"You already found one. I'm CPR/AED current and a National Academy of Sports Medicine CPT."

"What the hell are you doing *here?*"

He burst out laughing.

"What do you charge?" she asked.

"For you? $15 bucks a session."

"You're on. Let's start Friday."

"You sure?"

"Yep. Man..." She looked around her. "This place is a dump."

Ron cracked up. "Yeah. I know."

***

Sarah stopped by the dean's office again the following day in response to Dr. Smith's earlier emailed request. Lana was at lunch this time and across the room, Judy was on the phone.

"Hello Sarah, I'm sorry I missed you the other day, I had to run out unexpectedly. Lana told me you'd stopped by." The two shook hands. "Have a seat," the dean invited.

"Hi Dr. Smith. Nice to see you. It's been a while."

"Sure has, sure has. As always, your evaluations are solid, and on par with the university. All the students rave about you. We're delighted to have you teaching for us."

"Thank you, Dr. Smith. Kind words always mean a lot."

"Having said that, would you be interested in taking on some additional classes for next semester? You fit so well here, and I think the students would really benefit, were you to be the teacher."

"I'm flattered Dr. Smith. Can I think about it for a few days? I'm in the process of making some changes, and I'd want to make certain everything works before I commit."

"Absolutely, Sarah. You actually have nearly a month before we need a decision."

Sarah stood and the two shook hands again. "Thank you," she replied.

"Don't work too hard," the dean joked.

"Likewise," Sarah smiled.

Chapter Three

Way of the World (Or Is It?)

Sarah had eventually met a nice-looking guy at the gym. She didn't think it would turn into anything serious, but you never knew how these things were likely to turn out. He told her he was in the process of starting a new business with his brother, and as was true with most start-ups, money was tight, so he really wasn't able to do much in the way of traditional dating.

He dressed well, spoke well, and he drove a well-maintained year-old BMW. Sarah liked the idea that he was an entrepreneur, and she didn't feel the need to be wined and dined and pampered, particularly if the guy was knocking himself out trying to start a new business. Regardless, the two of them were compatible, and occasionally she'd let him sleep over at her place.

Ed took notice of the occasional overnight presence of the beemer.

One evening Ed and Sarah were comfortably ensconced in white plastic chairs in front of the crackling fire pit, each nursing a rum and coke.

"Who's the guy I see staying with you once in a while?" Ed asked.

"Name's Phillip. Why?"

"What's he do all day?"

"Specifically? I have no idea. He said he and his brother are partners in a start-up. Never got around to asking for details. Something to do with online marketing, I think."

"I'm calling my buddy Jack to do a background check."

"What?"

"I'll need your guy's full name and as much information you have on him before you leave tonight if you're going out. Full name, phone number, address, where you met, whatever you have. I want to get it to Jack so he has it first thing in the morning."

Sarah rolled her eyes and giggled. "OK, Daddy," she teased him.

"Well, girl, I'm going to call it a night," Ed said as he stood and stretched. "You want a 'go drink'?"

"Sure, why not." She rose and followed him inside, casually leaning against the kitchen counter as he was dropping ice cubes in her glass.

While he was fixing her drink he reached over and grabbed a grocery list note pad and ballpoint then slid them toward her on the counter.

"Write the guy's name down and anything else you know about him."

She looked at Ed curiously but did as he requested. "Here you go. Let me know what you find. Now you've got *me* curious."

Ed handed her a fresh rum and coke and walked her to the door.

"Call me if you need me," he said, then shut the door after her.

Sarah raised a hand and waved a backward goodnight, then walked back to the camper. Instead of going straight inside, she sat on the steps for a few minutes and enjoyed the star-filled night sky.

Well. That was interesting, she thought.

I wonder if this is what a father daughter relationship is like. Wish to hell I'd had this kind of thing with my own father when I was growing up. This protective attitude is kinda' nice.

***

OK, Sarah thought happily when she woke up. *No classes today. Got a day just for me. I'm going to drive into Raleigh and hit the gym.*

Sarah eyed herself in the mirror. She liked what she saw today. She wore a new L.L.Bean™ outfit that she considered casual chic, and it simply made her feel good.

As an afterthought, she gave her neck a light spritz of Chanel's Coco™. *Expensive as hell but I love this scent,* she thought as she headed for the car.

As the local gas station hove into view, she decided she wanted a cup of coffee for the rest of the drive. She pulled in, parked, and opened the door. She hailed the station's owner, Shaniqua O'Brien, as she headed for the coffee bar.

Shaniqua was smart as well as pretty. She had been blessed with a flawless caramel latte complexion, greenish hazel eyes, a knock-em-dead figure, and softly curled chin length dark brown hair. While Shaniqua had majored in theatre, she'd given her choice of a future career a lot of thought.

Her extended family was in North Carolina, she didn't particularly want to travel any more than she already had, and she wanted to become financially secure. She decided to work with a local studio that filmed reasonably priced but professional looking commercials for national clients. It was part-time work, it paid well, she saved her money, and she invested it. Shaniqua now owned two small gas stations and a laundromat with machines you could operate by using PayPal™ instead of carrying around a load of quarters. The girl was smart as a whip.

"Hey Shaniqua! How're you doin'?"

"Hey yourself, girl, how you been?"

"Hangin' in my friend, hangin' in. What's new with you?" Sarah asked as she poured herself a large coffee, snapped the top on the insulated paper cup and headed for the register.

"Met somebody interesting, goin out with him tonight for the first time."

"Cool beans! What's he do for a livin?"
"College professor."
"No shit? He's at the university? What's his field?"
"Got his doctorate in business administration."
"Dang, girl! You got a live one! Let me know how it goes."

"That I will!" Shaniqua smiled happily, then paused and sniffed the air.

"You just hop out of the tub?" Shaniqua asked.
"Uh-uh, I showered last night, why?"
"I smell Irish Spring soap."
"Say what?"
"Irish Spring. I smell Irish Spring soap," Shaniqua reiterated.

"Uh... I'm wearing perfume. It's Coco, by Chanel. Maybe that's what you sm..."

"Lean over, lemme take a sniff," Shaniqua suggested as she finished ringing up the coffee.

Sarah leaned halfway across the counter and Shaniqua leaned forward and sniffed. "Yeah. You smell like soap. Smells good. Fresh scent. You smell nice and clean."

"Uh... thanks. Well... I... uh... I gotta run," Sarah said as she pocketed her receipt. She waved bye with her free hand. "Good luck with the new guy, Shaniqua," she called. "You guys have a nice time tonight!"

Sarah headed out the door, climbed in the car and just sat there for a good thirty seconds.

Did this conversation actually just happen? This fucking perfume cost me a hundred forty-eight dollars and nineteen damn cents for a freaking thimble full. And I've just been told it smells like a goddamn bar of soap. Am I missing something here?

She shook her head, started to laugh, and started the car.

Soap. I smell like soap.
My life is so weird.

She pulled out of the parking lot, got back on the road, and started laughing all over again.

***

Sarah was keeping herself busy. Working hard teaching, and training hard with Ron, who as it turned out, was just coming out of an unpleasant divorce.

Today he had Sarah doing lunges back and forth in the main room of the gym.

"C'mon, Sarah, two more, you can do it."

"Fuuuucckkkkk. Damn. I am *not* having a good time with these, Ron."

He tried to hold in a laugh but failed miserably.

She did another lunge. "Hey, are you doing OK with your divorce?"

"So, so." He shook his head. "Women," he sighed. "The marriage just wasn't working for either of us. No point in dragging it out."

"It gets better. If you need anything, let me know."

Sarah paused to catch her breath.

"Thanks. What are you doing for Thanksgiving?" he asked curiously.

"Probably spending it with Ed. He's kind of like my adopted dad. He took me in."

"How 'bout you?"

"Dad, stepmom, and brother. Dad's deep-frying a turkey. Want to come over?"

"I've never had deep fried turkey. Sounds interesting, though. Since you're a body builder guy, I trust you'd know whether it's any good or not."

Ron smiled, rolled his eyes, and Sarah laughed. "OK, yes, thank you for the invitation. I accept."

"Cool. OK, back to lunges."

"Crap. Here I was hoping all the turkey talk would make you forget about the lunges. Man, look at me. I'm dripping wet. I'm probably sweating out all the rum I've been drinking."

***

Ed was at his desk when he heard the sound of tires as Sarah's car turned off the main road and headed down the rutted driveway into the compound. He was dialing Sarah's cell phone before she even had a chance to park. She pulled up next to the camper, parked and shut the engine off, then reached for the phone. The name *Ed* appeared in the caller ID window.

"Hey, Ed. What's up, sweetie?"

"Hey, girl. Can you come over for a minute? I wanna talk to ya."

"Sure. You, OK? Is everything all right?"

He ignored the question. "Door's open. I'm in the kitchen. Come on back."

Click.

"That man *never* says goodbye," she laughed to herself.

She walked over to the house, tapped on the door to let him know she was on her way in, yelled, "It's me." Then she wandered on back to the kitchen where Ed stood at the counter, adding a couple cubes of ice and a splash of Coca-Cola™ to a rum and coke. He had a cigarette in his mouth, as usual.

Ed called over his shoulder. "Want a drink?"

"Am I gonna need one?" she teased. "I just finished working out, but why not? Make it a small one please?"

He nodded approvingly. "Remember what I always tell ya, maintain your buzz, but never get drunk."

"You're a good influence on me."

He smiled. "So listen, you still seeing that guy Phillip?"

"He's been out of town for the past couple of weeks visiting family. S'posed to get back in town this afternoon. Said he'd call me when he got in."

Ed fixed a small rum and coke for Sarah and carried both glasses over to the breakfast bar in the kitchen. He grabbed one of the tall ladder-back stools and slid it away from the table before settling himself comfortably.

"Pull up a chair and sit down, girl." He waited until she had done so and had taken the first sip of her drink.

Sarah looked at him expectantly. She didn't know what was coming, but she suspected it was not going to be good news.

"Jack called. Don't shoot the messenger. You're a grown-up and you get to make your own decisions."

"Yeah, yeah. I get it. Give it to me straight, Ed. What'd he say?"

"He said that guy Phillip owes over a hundred grand to the IRS. It's a judgment for back taxes."

"Say *what?* He asked me about my own debt, and I said I had some, and he said he didn't have any." She paused, looked over at him, raised an eyebrow and sighed despondently.

"There's more, right?"

"Yep. He's unemployed, and he's usin' the sailor method."

"What the hell is that supposed to mean, Ed?"

"He's got a gal in every port. In this case they're in nearby towns, just far enough apart not to run into each other at a grocery store. They think they're the only ones he's seeing. He'll tell them he's either traveling on business, or out of town for a job interview, any old excuse will do. He'll just come up with something that sounds plausible, when instead he's living with each of them on an impromptu rotating schedule. He's what we used to call a gigolo, only in his case he has multiple sugar mamas.

"He looks for attractive single women with no dependents, a steady job and good income. Age doesn't matter. He actually prefers older women because they tend to be more generous with him.

"Some he'll tell he's going through a divorce and that's why he has no money, others he might tell that a business partner screwed him and embezzled the money. His excuses sound valid, and he makes them sound good enough that the women not only don't ask him to pay for anything, but they also don't expect to be taken out on dates either.

"They buy him clothes, they give him pocket money, they take him places. Some give him a prepaid *visa* card so they're sure he's never caught short and able to keep up appearances should he ever be presented with a bill. He's real careful with those cards because there's a running record of how every penny is spent. He'll often use them to enhance the image. Maybe bring the women flowers, maybe pick up a bottle of wine for their dinner or buy gas for his car. His car is leased by the way.

"The women are always the ones who'll spend the money to buy the groceries and the booze. He'll say he's on his way back from a trip and he's exhausted, and he'd love a steak but he's short of cash. He'll offer to stop at McDonald's on his way home and bring burgers. It's the little things like that help set the scene.

"Nine times out of ten the women will typically rush to the grocery store and have steaks or shrimp or whatever he says he's been dreaming about, ready to grill when he gets there.

"In short, the guy is a sweet-talking grifter who takes advantage of women. One of the women he's seeing is even paying for the lease on his car."

Silence.

Sarah shook her head. "Son of a bitch. I fell for it. I actually bought into his line. I swear to you, Ed, I thought I was smarter than that."

"You gotta' be careful girl. Do your homework. You have a lot to offer a guy. Beautiful, single, no dependents, great education, good job... A sweet talkin' grifter'll take advantage of that. It's better to know this shit up front."

Ed lit a fresh cigarette. For two cents Sarah would have asked him for a drag but she changed her mind. No point in backtracking just because the guy she'd been dating turned out to be a lying asshole.

"Shit," she said, with a heavy sigh, and a look of disappointment on her face.

"You were absolutely right, Ed. Better to find out about this stuff right up front."

"Well," she sighed again, viewing the bad news pragmatically. "I guess I'll go get outta' these sweaty clothes and take a nice hot shower. I'll holler at you later this evening. Thanks, Ed."

"No problem girl. Call me if you need me."

Sarah stood, drained the last of her rum and coke, carried the glass to the sink, then turned and headed for the foyer. Ed walked her to the door. She did a backward wave as she skipped down the steps and headed for the camper. Ed meant to casually shove the door shut, but instead managed to land a resounding slam. It startled Sarah, whose thoughts were elsewhere. The noise made her jump about a foot in the air.

Why does that silly sumbitch always do that? She shook her head and laughed out loud.

Shit, she thought again as she replayed in her head what she'd just learned about Phillip. *Jeezus,* she reflected, as the obvious just hit her right between the eyes. The potential for having caught an STD from him had just multiplied exponentially. *Gonna have to schedule a checkup. Fucking asshole.*

Ten minutes later her gym clothes were in the tiny bathroom hamper, and she was standing in the shower, letting the warm water run over her face and hair as she leaned against the shower wall. She took another deep breath.

Well... It is what it is. Fuck.

A half hour later Sarah was sitting on the sofa in her bathrobe, a towel around her wet hair, dialing her phone. There were three calls that needed to be made. Might as well get 'em over with.

Here we go. First of three calls. He answered on the first ring.

"Hi Phillip. How are you?"

"Hey sweetie. I just got back from visiting my family. I had a great trip. I missed you baby."

He had the phone on speaker so he could casually scroll through the new photos on the phone as they spoke. He was looking at pictures of girls he'd met while visiting his family.

"We need to talk Phillip."

"Is everything OK? How about I come over in a couple hours. In the meantime, you can run over to the store, pick up a couple steaks and I can grill them. And oh yeah, don't forget we'll need a couple six packs of beer and a can of green beans."

"Excuse me? What did you say?" Sarah flashed back on what she had just learned about the way Phillip got women to buy things to please him. For a moment it was like waving a red cape in front of a bull, then she decided to take a different tack. Maybe have some fun with it. Maybe turn the tables.

"Lighten up sweetie. I'll see you soon," he said.

"Wait, don't hang up, Phillip. I need to tell you something important. I can't see you any more."

"Sarah, sweetheart, you don't mean that. I love you, honey, and you know that I'm the best lay you've ever had."

"Bless your heart, Phillip, in all honesty you're just a point or two above average, but you truly are awfully sweet, and that more than makes up for the rest of it. But it just wouldn't be fair to you, under the circumstances..."

The 'just a point or two above average' really hit him where it hurt.

He struck back, "Just so you know, your pussy smells like parmesan cheese with an Italian twist."

She was finding it very difficult to keep up the charade after that comment. She literally had to choke back the laughter.

"Wait a minute..." he suddenly said. "What do you mean by 'under the circumstances.' What are you talking about?"

"Oh, sweetheart, that's what I called to tell you. You probably need to schedule an appointment with your doctor right away. And if you've been seeing anybody else, you'll need to tell them to get checked as well. Whatever you do, don't wait. This is one of the bad ones. I'm told that it's a new strain that can't be killed with current antibiotics. Take care, Phillip, and again honey, *please* don't wait. The risk to your health is far too great."

Phillip totally lost it. He began screaming so insanely that he was spitting as he was shouting. Sarah held the phone a foot away from her ear and had to hold a couch pillow up to her mouth to muffle her laughter.

"What the *fuck?* You miserable goddamned bitch! You exposed me to gonorrhea? To H014? Are you insane, you fucking whore? You gave me gono..." She smiled as she hit disconnect mid-rant and permanently blocked his number.

Pleasant dreams, Phillip. She burst out laughing then rolled her eyes.

Parmesan cheese with an Italian twist? That's a first. I've never had any complaints about my pussy before, you lying dickhead.

Second phone call. She glanced at her watch. The office was still open. She went ahead and dialed.

"Hi Carolyn, Sarah Watson. Does Dr. Tyler have any openings in the near future? Yep, I'm well, thanks. I just want to schedule a check-up. Broke up with a jerk, want to make sure all is well before I consider dating anybody else. Cancellation? Sure, I'll take it. Tomorrow at two works fine. Great, see you guys then. Nope, not pregnant. No, no warts. Have a great day."

Sarah disconnected the call but sat there staring at the phone. "But I might smell like a fucking Italian sub." She burst out laughing.

OK, third call. This one was to the dean.

"Dean Smith please, this is Sarah Watson. Oh hey, Lana, how you sweetie? Sure I'll hold."

"Dean Smith? Hi, Sarah Watson here. How are you? Great. Listen, I'm not going to need a month to make a decision after all. Already cleared my schedule and I can pick up four classes for the coming semester. Yeah, it's OK. No problem. I'm looking forward to it. OK thanks. Take care. Bye."

"I really do work too much," Sarah sighed.

Sarah dried her hair, considered cooking something but settled on a peanut butter and jelly sandwich instead. She pulled on a comfortable old sweat suit, gym socks, slipped on a pair of tennis shoes and her Little Red Riding

Hood snood, picked up the phone and invited herself over to Ed's to sit out back by the fire with him.

When she arrived, Ed was neatly arranging firewood in the pit and liberally drenching the logs with a can of charcoal lighter fluid. He flicked on one of those long-handled BBQ grill lighters, squeezed the trigger, and watched as fire obediently roared into existence.

Sarah pulled up one of the white plastic chairs and stared morosely at the newly roaring flames.

"I shoulda' brought marshmallows and a coat hanger," she sighed to Ed.

"You'll find a bag of marshmallows in the pantry, if you're serious," he offered, as he settled himself into the chair next to hers.

She considered it for a moment. "Nah, I don't think toasted marshmallows go all that well with rum and coke," she decided. "But thanks for the offer," she smiled.

The pair sat in companionable silence.

"Your car paid off yet?" he asked suddenly.

"Not yet."

"Credit cards?"

"I'm workin' on it, Ed. I just signed on to teach some extra classes next semester. That ought to speed things up some."

"You OK?" he asked.

"Yeah, sorry. Bad day."

She sat quietly, deep in thought.

"Need any money until payday?"

"No, I'm OK, thanks."

"Did you break it off with that guy?"

"Yup. Sure did."

"That's an important life lesson. You need to be careful girl. You gonna finish moving into the little cracker house this weekend?"

"I need to see if your handyman can help me move a few boxes. I can pay him ten bucks an hour or a guaranteed ten minimum if it takes less than that."

"I'll tell him you need him for an hour or so this weekend."

"Thanks."

***

The following day, Sarah sat in the waiting room of her gynecologist.

The physician's assistant stood at the door with a clipboard.

"Sarah?" she called.

"That would be me."

"C'mon back."

"How're you feeling? The nurse asked, as the two of them walked toward the exam room."

"Feel fine."

"Any problems?"

"Nope. Just here for a checkup."

Halfway back the nurse paused in a wider part of the hall. "OK, just go ahead and set your purse on the chair and step on the scale so I can check your weight."

"I have to stand backwards." Sarah explained. "I don't want to know my weight."

"Uh... OK." The nurse looked slightly startled, but indulged her request. "You're in great shape. You could eat a pound of cookies a day for an entire year and you still wouldn't have a thing to worry about."

Good to know, Sarah thought.

"Thanks," she replied.

"OK, we're going to room two," the nurse told her. "You know the drill. There's a changing booth in the corner. Take off everything and put on the paper gown. Leave your shoes on if you want. When you're ready just have a seat on the examination table and the doctor will be right in."

What if I do smell? Sarah worried. She grabbed a paper towel and wet it at the sink in the exam room, quickly giving herself a quick swipe before using the step-on pedal that opened the red can. She tossed the paper towel, and then perched on the edge of the exam table.

There was a knock on exam room's door, the doctor's way of giving the patient a head's up before he entered.

"Hi Sarah."

"Hello, Dr. Tyler." The nurse followed him into the room and stood at the side of the exam table. The nurse draped a paper blanket over Sarah's lap, then instructed her to lie back and insert her heels in the leg rests.

The doctor rolled a short stool over and sat down, gave her a quick professional exam, and within less than sixty seconds reported that everything looked fine. No problems.

"Any concerns or questions?" he asked her.

"Matter of fact yes," she replied. "Can I ask you something a little strange, since you have a front row seat, as it were?"

"Sure," he said. Go ahead."

"Do I smell like parmesan cheese with an Italian twist?

The doctor scooted the little black stool back, a bemused grin on his face, looked her in the eye and asked, "Pardon me?"

His nurse, on the other hand, was literally convulsing with laughter.

"Yeah," Sarah explained. "I just broke it off with I guy I accidentally learned was a total asshole, and he lobbed that little gem at me before I hung up on him. I just wanted a second opinion."

Dr. Tyler smiled and shook his head. "Forget it. The guy's an asshole. Everything's fine."

"Thanks for answering my bizarre question. Welcome to my world."

Chapter Four

Living (I Think)

I swear I don't remember having this much stuff when I moved in here. This damn camper is the size of a postage stamp. Where did I ever even put all this crap?

During an earlier run a number of days ago Sarah had transported several boxes to the empty cracker house, chief amongst them were the two good-sized boxes which had contained bottles from the liquor cabinet. The experience made it clear that an additional pair of hands, a strong back, and a pickup truck would make the moving drill a whole lot simpler.

She looked at the cardboard mountain in the camper's little living room. Ten freaking boxes, all taped up and ready to go. She shook her head in amazement at the sheer amount of stuff there was. To be perfectly honest, there actually was a good reason for the additional bulk. She'd been gradually accumulating household stuff, getting ready for the move to an unfurnished house. Some of the new things she'd bought were kitchen appliances, sheets and towels, cookware, tableware, broom, mop, portable vacuum, that sort of thing.

A moment later, there was a knock on the door. She glanced out the little window in the door and could see Ed's handyman Robert standing at the base of the steps. "Y'all got some shit needs movin'?" he yelled.

Robert frequently boasted that he was a genuine redneck. His busted ass rusty pickup truck proudly flew a large Confederate flag and the truck's tailgate boasted a two-foot-wide vinyl sticker insisting The South Will Rise Again. The bumper held a faded yellow tea party sticker. Robert had long greasy hair, at least half of his original teeth, and he chewed tobacco. Sarah assumed he was somewhere near middle-aged. Being around him literally set Sarah's teeth on edge.

For the life of her, Sarah couldn't come up with a single reason why Ed would have hired Robert in the first place, but Ed usually had a good reason for everything he did. That didn't mean Sarah had to put up with Robert's bullshit, though. She was only hiring him to move some boxes in his truck.

Sarah opened the door. "Oh, hey Robert."

"Ed said you needed help moving a few boxes to the cracker house?"

"Yes sir. I appreciate you coming by to give me a hand. Thank you."

"So you're staying huh? Didn't think a citified lady like you would last a week out here."

"Well, I did, and here I am. You're on the clock now Robert, so if you'll just take these boxes and load up the truck, we can get this done."

Robert obediently grabbed one of the boxes and headed for the truck.

Sarah loaded clothing into her own car, figuring it had a far better chance of arriving clean and undamaged that way.

The move actually went reasonably smoothly. Sarah politely thanked Robert for his help and slipped him a twenty, even though it only took him about forty-five minutes. In her eyes it was well worth the extra ten to get rid of him quickly.

Sarah was making good progress with the unpacking and had stopped for a short break when she glanced out the window and caught sight of Ed approaching the side door.

"Door's open," she yelled. "Come on in, Ed!"

"Hey, girl," he said as he looked around, "You're gonna need you some furniture!"

"Hey yourself, Ed. I'm gonna sleep on the old sofa the other tenant left behind until I can afford to buy an actual bed."

Ed shook his head. "I know the owner of a discount furniture store over on Williams Street. We can go over there tomorrow. Remember, this is North Carolina. They actually manufacture furniture here. Real cheap prices. Besides the store has free local delivery."

"Ed, I honest to God can't afford to do that yet, and I don't want to purchase anything else on credit. I'm still trying to pay my cards off. I'm also trying to get the car paid off too."

"Don't worry about it, girl. What time will you be up?"

"I don't know Ed. I'm supposed to go to a party tonight."

"With who?"

"Just meeting some friends over at the biker clubhouse."

"Be careful."

"Always. Besides, I don't plan to stay there very long anyway."

"OK, then give me a shout when you wake up tomorrow. We can go over to the furniture store then."

Sarah walked to the side door with him and waved bye.

What the hell. Couldn't hurt to look. At the very least it'll give me an idea of what I should budget for.

***

There was certainly no question about it being a party. Bikes were roaring, music was blasting. The closer Sarah got to her destination the louder the din became. She was in a good mood, rocking out, singing along with the radio in her car until she finally had to shut it off. It was totally overpowered by music coming from the party.

She had turned off the main road and was following the line of bikes and cars onto a private road. An adjacent field was being used for parking. She pulled off the pavement and parked on the grass in the ragged line of cars and bikes. It reminded her of parking for football games.

Sarah had chosen her outfit carefully. She had on a pale pink strapless bra under a white tank, tight black jeans with a black leather belt, a lightweight black windbreaker, and killer red stiletto heels. Simple, but hot looking, especially with her shoulder-length, softly waved blonde hair worn loose.

There was a good reason for parking as close as she could possibly get to the paved surface of the private road. Attempting to traverse more than five feet of a grass field in an expensive pair of stilettos was akin to suicide. For the shoes, that is.

Sarah was actually prepared for a worst-case scenario. She routinely kept a couple pair of topless black sandals in the glove box and in the messenger bag she used for school. At a mere two millimeter thick, the self-adhesive, disposable foam soles had saved countless pairs of shoes from sudden rainstorms, flooded parking lots, or sinkable grass fields that could shear the leather surface off a pair of stilettos in two seconds flat. She shut the car off, opened the door, and appraised the terrain. No problem. She had managed to park close enough to tiptoe from the car to the pavement wearing the stilettos.

Sarah was traveling light. She had her driver's license, insurance card, a twenty-dollar bill and her *visa* card tucked in a back pocket of her jeans. She had planned to leave her phone under the driver's seat of the car when she went inside.

She made one last phone call. Big Lou saw her name pop up on caller ID and answered immediately. "Hey sweetheart. You here? Where are ya?"

"Just parked. I'm not gonna drag my phone in with me, so I wanted to find out where you were before heading in."

"Come to the main club house, doll. I'm at the bar."

"See you in a few."

***

Sarah walked into a large clubhouse filled with both men and women bikers, loud music and three separate bars. People were dancing, a couple of women were gyrating on stripper poles, some were at tables gambling, and laughing, and there were random shot contests taking place. Sarah paused at the main entrance to get her bearings as she scanned the crowd at the main bar for Big Lou.

A group of three beer-drinking bikers had been standing together talking, when one of them caught sight of her.

"Psst, head's up," Black Jack said to his companions, inclining his head toward Sarah as she came through the door. She waved at them but as one they silently turned their backs on her.

"Oh, hell, *now* what?" Quip moaned.

Annoyed, Black Jack asked in a low voice, "Why the fuck is she here?"

"I thought this was invite only," Sparrow mumbled with a frown. "Christ. If my old lady sees her here I'm gonna catch holy hell fer sure."

"Great piece of ass, but bitch, it ain't consensual sex if you shoot your big mouth off to my old lady afterwards," said Quip.

"Yeah, the bitch dimed me out too," confessed Black Jack.

"So, who the hell invited her?" Sparrow demanded a split second before the obvious answer hit him right between the eyes. "Oh mannn…" Sparrow winced. "It had to have been Big Lou. What the fuck does he see in her, anyway?"

The three looked at each other in silence, then burst out laughing.

"Well yeah… there was *that*…" they agreed.

But they'd each had to pay the piper, when for some totally unknown reason she decided to shoot her mouth off. She had slept with each of them once over maybe a two-month period and naturally, she'd been discrete. But one day she got drunker'n hell and when somebody pissed her off, she had blown the whistle on all three of them.

Boy that was an experience none of them would care to repeat, because the shit had really hit the fan with their wives. Bottom line, yeah, it might have been a helluva ride, but for the amount of grief they took, it just flat out hadn't been worth it.

"No point in complaining to Big Lou. He's the president and he obviously wants her here. And if we give Sarah a hard time, he might kick us out," Black Jack observed. "Then where would I go to screw around on my old lady?" he asked logically. The others laughed.

"Fuck it. Let's just ignore her and have a good time," Sparrow suggested. "Pretend like we don't even know she's here." There were nods all around.

"Good plan," Quip agreed.

***

Big Lou was watching for her and when she came through the door, he raised his arm and waved, giving her a big smile. She made a beeline for him and gave him a big hug. He returned the hug and kissed her on the cheek.

"I see you made it baby girl."

"Hell yeah, I wouldn't miss this for anything Lou."

He stood and took her hand, "Come on, take a walk outside with me for a minute."

The pair walked away hand in hand.

"Are we cool?" Sarah asked curiously, puzzled by the request.

They walked a little further, getting away from the bulk of the crowd, then he stopped, gently turned her around, put his hands on her shoulders and looked her dead in the eye.

"There are a few guys who'd prefer that you weren't here, but I'm sure you already know that. Probably the guys you fucked and kicked to the curb. But what I'm telling you is not common knowledge, so this is just between me and you, baby girl. I want you to promise me you won't get mouthy today. I stuck my neck out so you could come and enjoy yourself today. Deal?" He smiled and chucked her gently under the chin.

Sarah smiled back. "Deal. Can I at least dance on the pole and get naked, should I be inspired to do so?" she joked.

"Have fun. All I'm saying is don't piss off any of my guys off tonight or they'll probably throw my ass out and elect a new president," he joked.

"You have my word, Lou," she told him. "Now then... where's my drink? Oh yeah, one more thing, for God's sake please don't ask me about my family tonight. It makes me absolutely nuts."

He burst out laughing, slipped his arm around her waist and they headed back inside.

"We cool?" she asked him.

He tugged her close. "Affirmative. Now give me some sugar baby girl, and go have some fun."

She threw her arms around his neck, and they hugged deeply. It wasn't until later that the word he had just unconsciously used to confirm an answer to her question, slowly rattled around in her subconscious.

Out of curiosity she ran a quick search a few days later, attempting to determine which profession used that word the most frequently.

***

The party was in high gear, Sarah was standing at the bar, surrounded by bikers, with whom she was laughing and flirting. She had long since shed the black windbreaker, the bartender having kindly tucked it away behind the bar for her.

The DJ put on Bob Seger's *Old Time Rock and Roll* from the soundtrack of *Risky Business*, and everybody yelled, "*Yeah!*" So he cranked up the volume to ear-splitting level.

Sarah and another sexy blonde decided they wanted to dance on top of the bar, so the two of them laughingly called to the bikers, "Help us up! Help us up!" and willing volunteers bodily lifted them up.

Somebody yelled to the DJ to start the song over and this time he cranked the music up even louder. The two women used dance moves that played off each other and the crowd went absolutely wild.

Talk about sweating out my rum consumption, Sarah laughed to herself afterwards. *What a workout!* She headed outside to cool off and catch her breath. This time she took a pass on the rum. Her glass held straight coke with ice.

Looking around she saw Quip, Sparrow and Black Jack standing together, laughing and drinking and looking at bikes. It was dark, so they hadn't yet noticed her standing in the shadows.

"Shit," she said to herself, after coming to a snap decision. "This is not going to be easy, but it's gotta' be done."

"Hey, you guys?" she said tentatively.

The blood suddenly drained from the faces of all three of them and they looked as if their lives had just passed in front of their eyes. They quickly looked around, praying their wives were nowhere near.

They were ready to scatter when she hit them with her do-not-mess-with-me teacher voice. "Quip. Sparrow. Black Jack!" It was as if she had cracked a whip, and the three of them froze.

When they turned to face her the looks on their faces were at once cold, angry, hostile, and defensive.

"Thank you," she said evenly. "I won't keep you, but this needs to be said. I inadvertently caused a problem for each of you with people that you care about. That was not my intent, and I owe you an apology." She looked at each of them, one at a time. "I'm sorry," she said.

They knew she meant it.

The three turned and walked away without a word.

Sarah took a deep breath then headed for one of the tree stumps that doubled as outdoor barstools. She sat down, sighed heavily, and sipped her coke. From her present emotional vantage point, she took a good look at her situation and suddenly, she saw things with remarkable clarity.

I had a good time at the party, but this is not my kind of place, and these are not my kind of people. I've been doing a lot of self-destructive shit for far too long. Granted these guys were assholes and they were cheating on their wives, but nobody needed me to screw their lives up any further. Tonight, I did what I needed to do to try to make amends. And now, I'm outta here.

It's time for a change.

***

The following day, as planned, when Sarah awoke, she telephoned Ed and the two of them headed out to do some furniture shopping. Ed had a friend with a wholesale furniture store and another friend with a used furniture store. They planned to check out both places.

Ed was piloting his Cadillac Escalade toward the first of the two stores and Sarah was in the passenger seat. She had gotten back home from the party long before midnight, so she hadn't felt the need to sleep in this morning.

"How was your party?" Ed asked.

"Enlightening."

"Come again?"

"Well, I didn't drink too much, and I did have fun, but while I was there, I realized that I didn't really fit in with that crowd. I teach at a highly rated public university but most of the people I've been socializing with were people to whom education was something to be avoided instead of appreciated. They were people who were comfortable in low places. I wasn't.

"Actually, the only person that I could actually relate to was Big Lou, the guy who owns that biker bar I told you about. And to be perfectly honest, I don't think he fits in with those people either. He's well educated, intellectually sophisticated, and a decent human being who actually gives a damn. What he's doing with a biker bar I swear I haven't a clue. There's gotta' be an interesting back-story there, but I'm not sure he's ever going to open up and share it."

"You know…you're really good for my head, Ed," she said. "You're a good influence. Your advice is sound and I'm so very grateful for all your help."

He ground his cigarette out in the ashtray and flicked the butt out the window. Then he looked over at Sarah.

"I'm just telling you my experiences girl. Teaching you how to protect yourself. You have been selling yourself short though."

"I hear ya," she said, meeting his look with a smile.

Ed had suggested that they hit the discount furniture store first.

The two of them were walking through the showroom when he asked for a list.

"What all do you need girl?"

"The basics: bed, table and chairs, one night stand, and one end table. I actually wouldn't mind having a reading chair for the living room if we find a cheap one, but it's not a total necessity. I don't need a sofa. The sofa that's already there is in pretty decent shape and there's no point in wasting money on stuff that's not actually needed."

"OK," Ed said. "Here we go. Here's a king-sized bed complete with a mattress, headboard and footboard. That's actually pretty attractive." He tapped on the wood. It wasn't actually wood. It was molded plastic, but it certainly looked like wood.

"Try the mattress," Ed suggested.

She sat on the edge of the plastic covered mattress then leaned back. "Oh man, is that comfortable," she sighed with pleasure.

He looked at the price tag. "Damn that's cheap. And delivery with set up is included. Let's look at the other stuff here then we'll swing over to the used furniture store. Sometimes they get really good quality stuff in, and they sell it for next to nothing, which means something used might be a better buy than something new but of lesser quality."

"Sounds good."

A few minutes later they were back in the Escalade, heading for the used furniture store.

Just as Ed had predicted, the used furniture store had multiple pieces of higher quality tables and chairs at prices both of them considered a steal. There was a warehouse section in the rear of the storefront, so the place actually had a huge inventory from which to choose.

"Ed," she protested again. "I'll look, but I can't afford to buy anything right now, and I no kidding definitely can't let you spend money on me. I really can't. I'm perfectly content to camp until I can actually afford to buy furniture."

Ed realized that Sarah was serious. She was tremendously uncomfortable with the very idea of him buying furniture for her, and he knew that this was a matter of pride, so he proposed an alternate solution.

"So, here's what I'm thinking," he said, as if this had been his idea all along. "It's often easier to rent a furnished house, so I'm looking at furnishing the cracker house as an investment. I'm also hiring you as the decorator. I will compensate you for your decorating services by renting you a furnished house at the price of an unfurnished house.

"I want you to choose what's attractive enough to make the place appealing not just to you, but to some future tenant. Don't skimp. Just use your common sense."

He watched the look on her face go from uncomfortable to enthusiastic. Her eyes actually sparkled at the idea.

She was going to get down to business. "OK... What's my budget?" she asked him.

"That's part of your job. You've now looked at the prices of things in two separate stores. You tell *me* what your budget should be."

Sarah grinned and ballparked a number.

"That's pretty cheap," he observed. "You think you can actually do the whole thing for that amount?"

"I think so. But just to be on the safe side, we'll plan on 10% for an unexpected cost overrun. How does that sound to you?" she asked.

"Works for me. Go for it. I'm going to go sit down while you shop."

Sarah grabbed a pen and small writing pad from her purse and pulled up the calculator function on her iPhone. She called the store owner over, instructed him to bring a sales pad and a pile of sold tags with him and to follow her around the warehouse. As they went, Sarah negotiated prices with him.

The used furniture store didn't carry mattresses, but they did have complete matching living room and bedroom suites that had come from luxury homes, so the bulk of what she selected came from the used furniture store, and the king-sized bed frame, mattress, two pillows, and a pair of king-sized sheet sets came from the discount furniture store. She had found everything she needed, including a particularly attractive area rug for the living room, and accent pieces for the walls.

All of their selections would be delivered at no charge, the following day. Sarah was happy as a clam and seeing her that way made Ed enormously happy.

"You know how much this means to me, don't you?" she quietly asked Ed as they headed for the parking lot.

He turned and looked her straight in the eye. "I know you've been on your own your whole life without any family support, Sarah. I know your self-confidence was shot for a long time, and your thought processes were pretty self-destructive. I've watched you make changes. You're still doing that. It does my heart good to see you getting your act together.

"I never married, never had kids. For some reason I guess I've come to think of you like the daughter I never had. I sure as hell can't explain it. It just happened. So, I don't know, I guess I instinctively feel fairly protective of you.

"Why do you think I ask about your friends, and your boyfriend, your family, your job? That's what fathers do. Not everyone is going to abandon you, Sarah.

"I know I can't keep you under my wing forever, but as long as you're with me I can watch out for you, and I'll still be there for you, even after you've left the nest. That's a promise."

Sarah tried very hard to blink back tears, but they threatened to overflow anyway. She stopped walking and hugged him for the first time.

"Thank you, Ed. You're changing my life."

He kissed the top of her head. "OK, girl, you can turn off the waterworks. Let's go home and make us a drink. Then maybe you can explain where we're gonna put all this shit we just bought." Sarah wiped her eyes with the back of her hand and burst out laughing.

***

Sarah stood in her living room and smiled at what she saw. The furnishings she had chosen made the little cracker house look like a real home, and that fact alone made her happy.

To be perfectly honest, she'd just as soon have spent Thanksgiving at home, but she had already committed to going to Ron's parent's place to have deep fried turkey for Thanksgiving. She wasn't wild about the idea, but what the heck.

She was dressed and ready to go, when she decided to call Ed.

"Hey, Ed. Happy Thanksgiving!"

"Hey, girl. What time you leaving?"

"In a few minutes."

"When are ya coming back?"

"Later this afternoon. I don't anticipate staying long."

"Call me if you need anything."

"Will do. I'll come by after I get back. We can go sit by the fire."

"Sally's bringing me a plate over this afternoon. I'll be here when you get back."

From what Sarah understood, Sally had been around nigh onto forever. She had started out cleaning house for Ed and eventually her services and income were revised to reflect the addition of mutually consensual physical relations. The arrangement had continued for a number of years and had eventually evolved into a genuine friendship as well.

***

Sarah watched for the address Ron had given her for his parent's house. When she located the house and saw the owners standing in the front yard, a thought struck her.

You can't tell a book by its cover.

Ron looked like a fairly normal guy. Ergo, she had expected to meet a reasonably normal family. *Whoo-boy. It ain't necessarily so,* she thought. Ron had recognized her car and waved. *Shit. Too late for me to call and say something came up and tell him I won't be able to make it after all.*

Three people were standing in the front yard, clustered around a thirty quart aluminum deep fryer with a welded stand and a portable propane tank.

The front yard, she cringed. *The neighbors must be thrilled.*

She parked the car, got out, and waved to Ron, who burst into a delighted grin.

"Happy Thanksgiving!" Sarah called as she approached. Ron gave her a peck on the cheek as a welcome, then made the introductions.

"Sarah, this is my dad, Steve, and this is my stepmom, Sharon. My brother Ted is on his way."

Sarah shook Ron's parent's hands. "Nice to meet y'all," she said, a smile frozen on her face.

Ron's father had apparently been a biker in his younger years. The weather was clear but still chilly, yet he was shirtless. Deeply tanned, he was thin as a rail. The tattoos, of which there were many, suggested that he might have been a member of Hell's Angels in the far distant past. A stringy gray beard reached to his navel, and there was healthy supply of grease under his fingernails.

Ron's stepmother, Sharon was also deeply tanned. The remnants of bleached blonde hair had gone to gray, and she looked like she'd been 'rode hard and put away wet' as the saying goes. Sarah figured the scrawny woman had probably done a fair amount of drugs in her day and that she was more than up to date on her current consumption of alcohol. The term 'pickled' came readily to mind.

At the moment Sharon, the stepmother had a bottle of liquor in her hand.

"Happy fucking Thanksgiving Sarah. Want a shot? Come on, Sarah."

"Oh, OK," she said politely, accepting a shot glass.

This is odd, she thought. *Ron is a health-conscious bodybuilder and here I am slamming shots at ten a.m.*

"Cheers," Sarah said and drank the shot.

"Let's do another, Sarah. Come on," Sharon urged.

Both did another shot.

Sarah puckered her lips. It was vile, whatever it was. "What is this?" she asked.

"Tequila," Sharon answered happily.

"Good stuff," Sarah said politely. "Thank you. Might I use your powder room for a moment please, Sharon?"

"Sure. Straight in, turn left in the hall, and the can is the first door on your left."

Sarah excused herself, barfed up the two shots of tequila, flushed it away, squeezed an inch of toothpaste onto her index finger to use as an emergency toothbrush, filled her cupped hands with cold water and rinsed her mouth. She returned to the group out front just as Ron's brother Ted was parking his Prius. Ron waved to him.

Ron's father, Steve was seated in one of the folding lawn chairs that were now arranged around the deep fryer. Sharon was setting up a folding table and hauling out a few more folding chairs.

Steve leaned back, lit a joint and took a deep drag. He slowly exhaled and smiled as he looked at the smoke that still hung in the air.

Turning to Sarah he asked curiously, "How do you know my son?"

"The gym. We workout together."

Ron's brother Ted slammed his car door, beeped it locked, then walked over to join the group. Steve stood and gave his son a hug. "Hey Ted."

Ted looked over at Sarah. "Hey Dad. Who's the broad?"

Excuse me? Sarah thought, her eyes widening slightly. But she responded politely to the asshole whose preppy attire might have been better suited for lunch at the country club than deep frying a turkey in the front yard.

Sarah extended her hand, and the asshole shook it. "Hi, I'm Sarah, a friend of your brother's. Nice to meet you."

He couldn't be bothered to respond. "I need a drink. Where's Sharon?"

"Already drinking," Ron responded.

"Oh boy," the asshole said, and walked away.

"Sharon, do you need some help with the table?" Sarah offered graciously.

"Shit yeah. You can pass out the paper plates and plastic knives and forks. We'll use paper towels instead of wasting the napkins."

Sarah smiled wanly and began to distribute the picnic style place settings on the folding metal table. *I'll assume that we're using the good paper plates today,* she thought sarcastically.

***

Sarah had run a search for deep fried turkey the prior evening. The articles were enlightening, to say the least. The number of Darwin awards that could be handed out to first timers was actually quite startling. Fortunately, the deep-fried turkey exercise in the front yard here had transpired without the bird either blowing up or catching on fire, both of which happened fairly frequently, according to what she had read.

The folding metal table, covered with a plastic tablecloth, now held the turkey, which Steve was currently carving, in addition to a bowl of stovetop stuffing, and a can of cranberry sauce which had been unceremoniously dumped un-sliced, on a small plate. There was also a bowl of instant mashed potatoes, and a smaller bowl of freshly microwaved frozen green peas. The table held five: Sarah, Ron, Sharon, Steve, and Ted.

"Don't be shy Sarah. Help yourself," Steve instructed as he passed her a serving plate full of turkey with a sharp fork balanced on top. She selected a small piece of white meat and passed the plate to Ron, who sat next to her.

"*Fuck!*" Sharon suddenly shouted: "I forgot the gravy. Fuck it! Hey, let's do a shot! Come on Sarah!" Sharon struggled to stand, then turned, intending to retrieve a bottle sitting on the grass near the deep fryer, but tripped and landed on her butt. Sharon quickly scrambled to her feet and traversed the distance unsteadily, returning to the table with a half-full bottle and Sarah's shot glass. She stumbled again but managed to pour a shot and deposit it on the table in front of Sarah.

Unwilling to appear rude, Sarah smiled and raised the shot glass. "Cheers. Happy Thanksgiving."

"I should go get a fresh bottle," Sharon announced blankly, as she stood there with a half-full bottle already in her hand.

Steve rolled his eyes. "Fer chrissake Sharon, jes' siddown wouldya?"

"Don't tell me what to do Steve," she snapped petulantly.

"God dammit Sharon, it's a holiday. Can you please slow down for once? You'll have Ron's friend drunk before noon."

"Not my fault," Sharon said defensively. "She drank those shots on her own."

Sharon attempted to navigate her way back to her chair, stumbled but caught herself this time. She sat with a thump and poured herself another shot.

"Sorry Sarah," Ron apologized quietly.

"It's OK, Ron."

"Why are you here with my family anyway," Ted asked Sarah belligerently.

Startled, she looked up. "Excuse me?"

"Ted, shut up man," Ron glared at his brother.

"I just find it odd that you're not spending the holiday with your own family instead of imposing on someone else's family," Ted remarked rudely.

Sharon tried to stand again, knocking her chair over in the process. "Sarah, want to wrestle? Let's wrestle Sarah. Come on. Wrestle with me."

Sharon staggered toward Sarah and collapsed on her lap. "I'm not gay or anything, I just want to wrestle."

Ron spoke sharply. "Sharon, quit."

Sharon rose from Sarah's lap and assumed a wrestling position. "Come on Sarah," she demanded.

Steve was disgusted. "Sharon you stupid bitch, you're insulting Ron's guest and you're embarrassing the rest of us. You never know when to quit. This family is a fucking mess." He leaned back in his chair and lit another joint.

There's my cue, Sarah thought gratefully, and rose from her chair. "Ron, I really do need to go back and spend some time with Ed," she said softly.

Addressing the others, Sarah said, "Thanks for the food and drinks. Nice to meet you, Steve, Sharon, and Ted."

Ron rose with her, walked Sarah to her car and turned to face her. He was embarrassed beyond words. "I… God, I am so sorry, Sarah."

"It's OK, Ron, it was fun. I'll see you at the gym."

As she drove away, she sighed heavily, and her eyes began to water. A tear rolled down her cheek. *Well,* she sniffed and brushed the tear away. *That was almost as awful as spending time with my own family.*

I need to go see Ed, she realized. *He's my real family.*

***

Sarah and Ed sat next to each other, gazing at the crackling logs in the fire pit, each nursing a rum and coke.

"So how was Ron's place for dinner?"

Sarah whimpered and rolled her eyes. "I don't want to talk about it."

"That bad, huh?"

"Beyond your wildest imagination."

"How's your furniture?"

"It's perfect, Ed. Absolutely perfect. Thank you again."

"Did your family call ya today?"

She shook her head. "No, they never do."

She sighed and drained the drink in her travel cup.

"Well, I think I've had about as much fun as I can take for one day, Ed. I'm gonna call it a night. See ya tomorrow, sweetie. Thank you for the drink. And the company. Especially for the company," she smiled.

Chapter Five

Time for Change (Not Yet)

Sarah crawled into her comfortable new king-sized bed and lay there, staring at the ceiling.
I truly love Ed for all he's taught me and done for me. But I'm still struggling to figure out what I need to do to get my act together. Sometimes it feels as if it's staring me right in the face but then it slips away before I can grasp it.
I feel like I need to change something, but I still haven't figured out what. It's time I started thinking about that for a while, I guess.

Sarah was in her classroom, and she should have been concentrating on the presentations her students were making so that she could grade them accordingly. The problem was that her attention kept wandering. Portions of their presentations kept fading in and out.
This is getting old. I hear the same thing over and over. I have inspired so many students over the years, but I've forgotten how to inspire myself. I've been teaching seven classes a term for six years. I'm burnt out.

Suddenly I hate this gig. Only reason I like it is because I run my own show. Maybe that's it. Maybe I need to be teaching something that will help expand my own consciousness.

I've taught at a major university for six years, going on seven. Maybe changing what I'm teaching could be the answer.

Oh shit. Her attention snapped back. *I have no idea what last two students said in their presentations. Lucky you. You're gonna get the benefit of the doubt today, kids.*

She gave each of them an A.

***

The days flew by, and Sarah found herself spending the majority of her free time with Ed. She found that he actually was good for her head. She began to ask herself what she really wanted to do with her life and realized that in being here she was actually accomplishing something important. She was being given the opportunity to start repairing years of mental and emotional abuse, both at the hands of her family as well as what she finally realized had to have been the emotional equivalent of self-inflicted wounds.

They spent a lot of time together, and in the process, they made a lot of memories.

At some point in the distant future, whenever she looked back, she would realize that this period of time remained vividly engraved in her memory. She could not only remember it, she could reexperience it.

The memories, preserved like vignettes in her mind, became her own private time machine.

Sarah and Ed had sat side by side in two of the set of six comfortable chairs that surrounded the circular fire pit in his backyard. The fire pit itself was close to five feet in diameter. It was surrounded by an eighteen inches high circular wall of bricks. A circular area of gravel surrounded the pit and that's where the chairs had been positioned. The full diameter of the gravel plus the fire pit was maybe twenty-five feet. She could see it in her head. She could hear the crunch of gravel under her shoes.

Between the chairs, Ed had placed sections of a tree trunk cut in two-foot lengths. They were from a huge old oak that had gone over in a storm years earlier. A big tree trunk. A good two feet wide. Ed had thought it a shame to simply have them turned into firewood, so they had become the equivalent of heavy end tables. Six of them. Both exposed ends had been sealed with clear polyurethane. A place to rest a drink, place a phone, a pack of cigarettes, maybe a bag of marshmallows. The fire was comfortably warm at that distance, the conversation was light and the both of them had laughed, simply enjoying the moment for what it was. It was a good memory. She visited it often.

Another time, when the two of them were sitting in front of the fire, they spoke of deeper matters. They shared moments from their respective lives. Told of people who had made an impression upon them, in one way or another. She remembered the earnest look on his face. The look in his eyes was memorable. It remained one of her favorite memories.

They had dinner together, each was a fairly proficient cook, and it was something they enjoyed. Sometimes they'd share the kitchen and cook together. And they'd laugh. They'd argue about which spices went better with what, and they'd experiment with different recipes. They'd sit at the breakfast bar on the tall ladder-back barstools in the kitchen, eating dinner and talking. Then they'd wash and dry the dishes together. He had a dishwasher of course, but they enjoyed the camaraderie of cleaning up. Then they'd sit and have an after dinner drink and talk some more.

Sometimes the two of them would sit in his den and they'd go over some of his company books. He explained some of the businesses he owned, how they worked, how they had come to be, and how he had gotten them to the point where they pretty much ran themselves these days. It was like tapping a hoop, he had explained. You watch, you gently guide their direction, and they keep on rolling. Understanding how things actually worked in business, broadened her horizons.

He'd present her with a business situation, ask how she would handle it, and then he'd explain whether her answer would or would not work, and explain why. She was effectively getting a hands-on crash course in business administration without actually realizing it. She loved to learn, and he loved to teach her. She remembered how fascinated she had been as she recognized similarities and differences in economies of scale. She told him about Shaniqua and her laundromat that didn't require quarters, and they talked about online businesses, and the way the economy looked to be headed. It had given her a whole different perspective on a lot of things.

Sarah and Ed were sitting out back, talking by the fire. They had previously discussed an investment Ed was considering and had compared notes on potential. He'd had his doubts, while she had felt strongly that it was a good idea. She had lobbied for him to make just a very small investment as a test. That was the night he told her that she'd been right and that he was so proud of her. What had meant the world to her was the pride she had seen in his eyes. She had learned from him. It was like... a father's pride.

Sarah and Ed had been at a diner and were just finishing their after dinner coffee. Ed had already added the tip and paid the bill. There was a young family in the next booth, a mom and two children, a girl, and a boy. The little boy had begun to choke, and the mother screamed. Sarah had seen a look come over Ed's face that she'd never seen before, it was if he had suddenly become an entirely different person. He literally vaulted over the table, shoved the mother and daughter out of the way, grabbed the little boy, looked to see if the airway could be cleared but it couldn't, so he immediately began the Heimlich maneuver. It takes only four minutes before a child experiences permanent brain damage. Ed knew what he was doing, and he saved the child's life.

Once he was certain the child was OK, he grabbed Sarah's arm, and quietly said, "Let's go."

Not a word was spoken on the way home. He knew she wanted to ask, and he also knew that she wouldn't. When they arrived home, he'd made no move to get out of the car. He just sat there silently, for thirty seconds. Finally, he said two words, "Vietnam. Medic."

And Sarah had responded with another two, "Thank you."

Another time, Ed, Sarah, and a new guy she had gone out with the first time, were sitting by the fire. Ed had invited them to stop by for an Irish coffee after the movie. The two men had talked for a while then Sarah said she had an early class and needed to call it a day. She stood, hugged the guy goodnight, told him that Ed would walk her to her little cottage next door. Of course, the guy had no choice but to say goodnight, get in his car and leave. Sarah and Ed remained standing until they heard his car pull away. Then they sat back down. Ed wordlessly shook his head *no*.

"Second cup?" he offered.

"Yep," she replied. And she diplomatically declined a second date with the guy.

There were other memories, of course. The two of them watching a movie together on TV, laughing at something while he was grilling a steak, Ed bringing her soup when she was sick... otherwise inconsequential instances which for some reason just stayed with her, simply because she had been genuinely happy.

***

Ed's phone rang. "Hey, girl, what's up?
"Ed, Ed, guess what? Can I come over?"
"Sure. Come on over. Door's open." She could hear him walk to the door and unlock it.
Sarah went excitedly tearing across the yard and ran inside.
"*I did it!* Ed, *I did it!* I'm debt-free! My credit cards are paid off and my car is paid off. Day-yum this feels *so good!*"
She threw her arms around Ed and hugged him. "Thank you so much, Ed. You got me doing the right stuff!"
Ed smiled.
"I knew you could do it. Want a drink to celebrate?"
"Sure, why not. Small one please."
"What else has been going on girl?"
Sarah sighed happily. "I quit hanging out with bikers, married men, liars, drunks, and everybody that's not good for my head."
"Making some serious changes, eh?"
"Yeah, but it's not always easy, Ed," she admitted. She stared at her drink glass thoughtfully.
"Ha!" he concurred. "Tell me about it."

They made small talk for a few more minutes until Sarah finished her drink. "I gotta go do stuff, but I was just so excited. The free and clear title to my car came in the mail, and my credit card statements came in, and each of them show a zero balance. I just felt so good that I wanted to share it with you."

She sighed happily again. "OK, enough celebrating. I've gotta go to the grocery store and then I need to grade papers. Need anything from the store?" she offered.

He shook his head no. "I'm good, but thanks."

"Thanks again, Ed. I'll holler at you later."

"Drive carefully."

Sarah finished grading papers then headed for Cary to do some shopping.

By the time she got back it was almost dark. Sarah pulled into her driveway with groceries in the trunk and a yoga book borrowed from the library. She popped the trunk and walked around to the back of her car.

"Hey girl," Ed called to her from the next yard. "Heard your car come in."

"Hey Ed! What are you doing, sweetie?" she asked cheerfully.

"Having a drink with Sadie."

Sarah heard the sound of Ed's back screen door open and lightly slam shut, and saw a figure descend from the steps to join Ed.

"Who?

Ed turned around and pointed to a pretty young mixed-race girl with shoulder-length fine textured straight black hair. Short, short dress, slit up the side, high, high stilettos. Sarah figured her to be in her early twenties, "This is Sadie," Ed said blithely.

Something clicked in Sarah's head, and she instantly put two and two together.

"Holy shit," she said to herself. Size zero, part-time 'working girl', built like a Kardashian, and dressed to kill. That dress and those shoes might look cheap on her, but they were definitely not inexpensive. *Good grief. I can smell her perfume all the way over here and she could swat flies with those false eyelashes. No subtlety there. This must be Sally's replacement. This little gal might be compensated to clean the pipes, but she's sure as hell not on the payroll to clean the house.*

"Hi Sarah," Sadie waved and called across the yard. "Ed's told me so much about you! How are you?"

"Oh, hey. I'm well. Sorry, gotta run, I have to put groceries away before stuff melts. Nice meeting you, uh… Sadie."

"Good night!" Sadie waved.

"Call me later girl," Ed suggested.

"Uh-huh. OK," she said with a wave. *Hoo-boy, I get that a man has needs, but damn, something a little less obvious certainly couldn't hurt.*

She passed on the invitation to call Ed later. She didn't want to chance interrupting anything.

Later that evening, Sarah was deep into introspection. The brief encounter with Sadie had prompted her to take physical stock of herself. She had been sitting on the edge of her bed, facing her image in the full-length mirror that was mounted on the back of the bedroom door. She sighed, then rose and stood in front of the mirror to take a better look.

I wear conservative clothes, mostly casual. I can't wear heels most of the time because I have to walk across campus then stand and lecture. Sarah pulled her shoulder-length hair up and wondered if the more sophisticated look made any appreciable difference. She put her arms back down and shrugged.

I'm slim. I have decent hips and boobs for a size six, but I obviously wouldn't be able to compete with somebody who was built like a brick outhouse. If massive boobs and a butt shelf you could park a pickup truck on is actually what a guy wants, I would definitely be out of the running.

She sighed. *I don't wear much makeup, just lipstick, a little blush, and occasionally some mascara. And I'll occasionally use a light spritz of perfume but nothing overpowering. I prefer the natural look. But if men want what I just saw on display over at Ed's house, I'm well and truly fucked. That's just not me.*

***

Christmas rolled around and Sarah could see Ed's Christmas tree on display through his big bay window.

She looked around her place. *Looks like a freakin' atheist lives here,* she thought to herself. No tree, no wreath, no lights. To be honest, she just didn't feel very celebratory at the moment. Sadie was a semi-permanent fixture at Ed's place for the time being, and that pretty much sucked the joy out of visiting.

Sarah had brought a new yoga book home from the library, with the intent to practice more advanced poses. It was not going particularly well. Wounded Peacock Pose was a bitch, and Formidable Face Pose was just fucking nuts.

Ed had been sitting at his desk, drinking and smoking. He picked up his phone and called Sarah.

The phone was on the floor next to her.

"Hey, Ed," she gasped.

"What are you doin over there girl?"

"Working on some advanced yoga, Ed," Sarah groaned and panted as she tried to catch her breath. At the moment she was stuck on the floor in a yoga move gone bad.

"Do what?" he asked.

"Never mind," she replied, gasping and panting some more as she attempted a Destroyer of the Universe Pose with one leg behind her neck and slipped.

"*Fuck it!*" she muttered and gasped audibly.

"What's that noise?"

"Nothing, you must be hearing things."

She finally stopped and sighed.

"Want to come over for dinner later?"

"Sure Ed. Who's cooking?"

"Either Sadie or me. Figure an hour."

Click.

Sarah stared at the phone. *Why does he always just hang up?*

An hour later Sarah walked twenty steps to Ed's house and knocked. Sadie answered the door, dressed in Ed's robe.

Well, that's a trifle informal for Christmas dinner, especially with a guest coming, Sarah thought to herself.

"Hey Sarah, come on in."

"Hello. Thanks. Where's Ed?"

"I think he's on the computer."

"Merry Christmas," Sarah said through a frozen smile.

"Merry Christmas from me and Ed," Sadie bubbled.

"Hey Ed," Sarah stuck her head in the den and greeted him.

"Hey girl!"

There didn't seem to be anything cooking for dinner in the kitchen, so Sarah asked, "Who's grilling?"

For a moment he looked confused.

"Oh shit! I am. Chicken. And there should be baked potatoes in the microwave. I need to turn it on."

"Make yourself a drink," he invited.

Sadie smiled. "Isn't he the best?"

"He sure is," Sarah agreed stiffly. There was a touch of frost on her reply.

"Ed, I need money for my hair and nails," Sadie reminded him.

"Later," he replied. "I gotta' grab the chicken off the grill. I got distracted. Might be a little bit well done."

He headed out the back door, pushing the start button on the microwave on his way out.

"So, Sadie, how old are you?" Sarah asked casually.

"I'm twenty-two."

"Great age. Great age," Sarah commented.

"Sadie get the table set," Ed called.

"OK baby," she called. "Sarah, will you help me?"

Sarah drained her drink. "Yeah, sure."

"Here we go." Ed carried a tray into the dining room with a plate of blackened chicken and a bowl holding three overly microwaved baked potatoes. The blackened part of the chicken wasn't a gourmet recipe. It more closely resembled a cremation exercise.

What the fuck? wondered Sarah. *The guy I know is a great cook.*

"Dig in," Ed invited.

"Looks great Ed," Sarah told him.

"Thanks baby," Sadie smiled.

"Would it be OK if we dimmed the lights, or just lit candles? It's really bright in here," Sarah observed.

"Sadie, light a candle and turn the light off," Ed instructed.

"Oh, that's much better, Sadie. Thank you. Merry Christmas, everyone," Sarah smiled somewhat stiffly.

Sarah managed to choke down two bites and never said a word about the chicken. She carefully sliced and rearranged it, spreading it out over the plate to make it look as if she had eaten most of it. Occasionally she'd take a very small bite of the over-cooked baked potato, just for effect.

"Well, I'm stuffed," she was eventually able to venture. "That was delicious Ed and Sadie. I'll clear the table and take care of the dishes." she volunteered.

Sadie simply left the table and headed for the TV. *Airhead,* Sarah thought.

"Thanks, Sarah," Ed said. "I've gotta' go make some phone calls. I'll call you tomorrow, girl. 'Night."

There was very little to clean up, so it took Sarah next to no time. When finished, Sarah walked to her little cracker house, and almost made it to the front porch before taking a short detour to throw up in the bushes.

Well, that was perfectly ghastly. Merry Fucking Christmas, she thought to herself.

***

Before anyone knew it the old year was gone.

Good riddance, Sarah thought with a sigh and a sardonic laugh.

But January had come and gone in a rush as well. *Boy... time sure seems to be quickly moving these days,* she thought.

On the plus side, it was the first Sunday in February, which across America meant *Super Bowl* Sunday. And that was usually fun. She'd been invited to swing by the home of an old friend to watch the game at her place. It would only be the two of them, her friend Molly explained, but it was always more fun to watch the *Super Bowl* with somebody else.

Sarah parked, grabbed a bag from the trunk and tapped on Molly's door.

Molly opened it and squealed with delight. "Sarah! Welcome."

"How are you? You look absolutely great, Molly!" Sarah gushed.

"Thank you! I've lost twenty pounds so far," Molly bragged with a giggle.

"Oh, here," Sarah handed Molly the tall gift bag. "I brought a bottle of wine."

"Thank you!" Molly said somewhat hesitantly, as she lifted the bottle out of the bag and glanced at the label.

"Oh, um... I ended up with surprise visitors, Sarah. My sister's family descended on me for a week so we're not going to be alone after all."

"That's OK, I can dash out and get another bottle or two. How many other people are there?" Sarah asked.

Molly winced. "My sister's a little nutzoid," she said in a lowered voice. "They're uber-religious. They don't drink."

"They won't have a problem if we do, though, right?" Sarah asked, joking.

Molly sighed and nodded. "Trust me on this. It's going to be much simpler to just avoid the drama these people are capable of creating."

"Not the end of the world, Molly. Don't worry about it. We'll just roll with it."

"The game is just starting," Molly told her. "Help yourself to the food, Sarah. We have tons. The dining room table is groaning under the weight of all this stuff."

"Thanks. I'm starving!" The two of them could hear cheering from the other room.

"I'll introduce you to everybody when the commercials come on," Molly told her.

"I can't wait for the commercials," Sarah quipped.

"They're the only reason I watch the game," she laughed. She didn't notice that Molly winced again.

Sarah quickly filled her plate and grabbed a seat in an empty recliner.

There are typically more than ninety commercials that air during the *Super Bowl*, amounting to roughly forty-nine minutes of airtime. But nobody really minds. That's because the commercials that air during *Super Bowl* are as much of a draw as the game itself. Every ad agency fortunate enough to have been chosen by an advertiser to create their commercial, vies to submit the best of the best, because that kind of exposure could mean a fortune in new ad agency business if their entry was well received, and winners earned a ton of free media coverage.

Sarah smiled and thought back. All these years later people were still talking about the hysterically funny, brilliantly clever, herding cat's commercial which had aired during the 2000 *Super Bowl*.

Somebody called time-out on the field and the station cut to a commercial. But just as that happened, the television itself went off.

Sarah blinked. "What just happened? Did the TV break?" she asked.

Molly's relatives laughed heartily at her question and Molly explained, "Ummm… no, Sarah, uh… we… uh… don't watch the commercials. It's the devil talking."

Sarah's jaw dropped. Molly shrugged an apology and inclined her head toward her sister.

"Well, God loves the horses on the *Budweiser commercials*," Sarah joked.

Nobody in Molly's family was even remotely amused.

"Please… Sarah…" Molly said, hoping for a peaceful afternoon without sparking a haranguing sermon from whatever strange religious group these people belonged to.

Sarah sighed. She figured it would be rude to walk out on her friend, so Sarah simply leaned back and made herself comfortable in the recliner and fell fast asleep.

Molly woke her when the game ended and whispered an apology. Sarah shrugged it off, thanked Molly for her hospitality, wished the bible thumpers well, and headed for her car. She stopped off at a friendly neighborhood tavern on the way home.

"Did you watch the *Super Bowl?*" the bartender asked, just making idle conversation.

Sarah laughed somewhat bitterly and nodded her head. "Yeah," she sighed. "But they wouldn't allow us to watch the commercials, and there was no booze," she said sadly.

The bartender felt her pain. He poured a rum and coke and set it in front of her.

"On the house," he said. "Whatever you had to sit through, I'm pretty sure you earned this."

Chapter Six

Unexpected Happiness (From Four Legs)

The festivities were over, and things were getting back to normal at the university. She had gradually tapered off going to the gym and rarely went there any more but decided to start using the indoor track at the school. While Sarah was warming up, she found herself observing the college-aged girls running the stadium. She shook her head and sighed.

Jesus, all of a sudden, I feel like I'm ancient. What am I doing here? I'm thirty something and stuck in a college town. She brushed the thought aside and began running. She made it two laps before experiencing the equivalent of an asthma attack. One of her students took note and rushed to her side to see if she was OK. Embarrassed, Sarah waved to signal that she was OK, then walked out to her car, got in, and shut the door.

She instinctively reached for the stale pack of cigarettes in the glove compartment. "Are you fucking insane?" she asked herself and slammed the glove box shut again. She started the car and headed back home.

As she drove into the compound, she saw a stray dog standing in the yard and immediately dialed Ed.

"Ed, whose dog is this out here? He looks mean. We need to call the dog catcher."

"I already did. Don't feed it or else it'll never leave."

"How am I supposed to get in my house? What if he's mean? Fuck's sake, it's always something. Hey, whose Corvette is that in your driveway?"

"Mine. Sadie talked me into trading the Caddy in for a Corvette. She said I looked better in a sports car."

"Oh, for fuck's sake," Sarah muttered under her breath.

"Don't feed that goddamn dog Sarah."

"Don't worry, I won't. Bye."

The dog was on the driver's side when she pulled into her driveway. He had followed her car.

Sarah sat in the car and stared at the dog. Big dog. Black Lab. He sat quietly, panting. Sarah crawled from the driver's seat to the passenger seat, hopped out, made a run for the door of her house and went inside. The dog never moved.

Sarah looked out the window. The dog wasn't where he was previously. *Good. He's gone,* she thought. She opened the front door and looked both ways. Nope. No dog. She took a few steps further and looked up and down the compound's road. *Great. He's gone.* She turned around to go back inside and found the dog sitting between her and the front door. His tail thumped happily.

He cocked his head.

"You're thirsty, right?" she asked him.

His tail began thumping again. "OK. I'll give you some water."

She went back inside and returned with one of her stainless steel mixing bowls full of water.

His whole butt was wagging as he drank. *OK, so we have a happy puppy response,* she thought.

"Are you hungry?" she asked him. Eyes bright, he looked at her expectantly.

"OK. Stay put. Let me check the fridge. I think there might be some leftover turkey from the deli."

His ears perked up.

"Aha! You know the word turkey, I see. All right. Hold your horses. Let me go check."

She came back with several slices of deli turkey on a paper plate and sat down in one of the chairs on her little front porch. "I'm only giving you this if you promise not to tell Ed," she told the dog.

He approached and shoved his head under her arm, encouraging her to pat him.

"OK, you're a good boy. Can you accept the turkey without taking my hand off?" she asked him.

He looked up at her and wagged his tail, then gently took a slice of turkey from her fingers.

"Damn. You really are a good boy, aren't you?" She leaned forward to pat him and he planted little wet dog kisses on her cheek.

Sarah fed him the rest of the turkey and he gave her more kisses. *Oh my God, I'm in love,* she thought. She threw her arms around him, and he was in dog heaven. He loved this woman. She gave him water and turkey and hugs. He would follow her to the moon and back. Has tail was wagging a mile a minute.

Sarah retrieved her phone and returned to the chair on the front porch.

She dialed Ed.

"Hey, Ed?"

"Where's the dog?" he asked.

"Cancel the dog catcher. He's sweet. I'm keeping him. And I'm naming him Charlie. Is that, OK?"

"Fine with me."

Click.

"You wanna come inside Charlie?" she asked him.

He walked to the front door and sat down, waiting for her to open it for him.

***

Sarah had plans for the evening. She and her friend Laura were going to hit a local club to go dancing. She was about to start getting ready and was waiting for Laura to arrive.

The phone rang.

"Hello?" Sarah answered it.

"Hey. It's me. I'm almost there. Are you ready?" Laura asked.

"I'm running a little bit late. I just adopted a dog."

"You what? We're still going out though, right?" Laura asked.

"Oh sure. Hurry up and meet Charlie."

"I'm almost to the turnoff for the compound. I'll be there in a minute."

Sarah had her robe on and had been just about ready to hop in the shower but decided to wait until Laura arrived so she could answer the door.

She sat down on the edge of the bed and Charlie snuggled up close, putting his head on her lap.

"God, but you're a sweetheart," Sarah said, kissing him on the top of his head. His tail began thumping again.

There was a knock at the door and Charlie went on full alert, giving her a questioning glance. "It's OK, sweetheart. That's gonna be Laura. Laura is our friend."

He followed her to the door and stood by her side as she opened it to admit Laura.

She leaned forward and gave Laura an air kiss and Charlie relaxed.

"*Oh,* he's beautiful!" Laura said, giving him a pat.

"Is he clean? Have you given him a bath yet?" she asked.

"Uhhh…"

"See if he'll get in the shower," Laura suggested.

"You wanna take a bath, Charlie?" Sarah asked.

Charlie bounced.

"I guess we'll take that as a yes," Laura said. "Turn the shower on."

"Wait, give me a second to get a bathing suit on if I'm gonna have to give him a bath," Sarah said.

Thirty seconds later, she returned in a bikini with her hair wrapped in a towel to keep it dry.

"OK, Charlie," she said as she turned on the water, grabbed the handheld showerhead and stepped into the shower stall.

"You coming?" she asked him.

He happily joined her. Good thing it was a decent sized shower. She adjusted the water temperature and wet him down, then grabbed the scented shampoo with conditioner and lathered him up. She could swear he was swooning with pleasure. Warm, soapy water, full coat massage, what more could a fella want?

Laura was laughing at the expression on his face. "Gawd he's cute," she said. "All right, get him rinsed and toweled off then take your own shower. We need to get rolling."

***

They left the clean, happy, and sleepy Charlie stretched out on a clean dry towel on the floor in the bedroom and headed out for the evening. Sarah left the radio on for him, so he didn't feel alone. She chose a mellow rock station with a DJ who had a soothing voice. They decided to take both cars.

The dance club was a popular one, the music was good, the drinks were reasonable, and the people pleasant.

"Are you having fun?" Sarah asked Laura. Both had taken a break from dancing with various partners to catch their breath.

"Oh boy, I've needed this for a long time. It's been nothing but nonstop work for months now, ever since I started the new business," Laura admitted. "I desperately needed a break," she told Sarah. "I never want to leave," she giggled.

Sarah: "I wonder how Charlie's doing?"

Laura grabbed Sarah off the stool. "He's fine. He's dreaming of hamburgers. Let's go grab somebody cute and dance!"

"OK, OK," Sarah laughed.

About fifteen minutes later Sarah had enough for the evening. She wanted to make sure Charlie was OK.

She waved off her dance partner and pleaded exhaustion, then approached Laura who had been dancing nearby. She had to yell over the music to make herself heard.

"I need to leave," she shouted.

Laura looked both incredulous and pissed.

"You're kidding me, right?" she demanded.

"I need to go check on Charlie. I'm not feeling this anyway. You stay and have fun. I've got a couch that turns into a bed if you want to come back to my place and stay over, but from what I can see, that guy you've been dancing with is waiting to rock your world."

Sarah nodded toward the guy and Laura turned and winked at him, prompting him to grin in return.

"You may be right," she said.

"Have fun, sweetie!"

Sarah walked out of the bar thinking, *I can't believe I'm leaving.* But she had no regrets.

An hour later, Sarah was nearly asleep when a voicemail tone came up on her phone. She opened one eye, looked at the message and smiled. Laura was staying at the guy's place and was not coming back for the night. She was following him back to his place. Laura's voicemail message gave Sarah the guy's name, address, phone number, and the tag number of his car. *Good girl, Laura,* Sarah thought to herself.

Sarah switched back to her home screen, then turned the phone off. With a sigh, she rolled over and found herself face to face with Charlie, who had quietly crawled up on the bed to sleep next to her.

"You better not be a blanket hog," she warned him. He gave her chin a small lick, sighed happily, and shut his eyes.

He snored. She didn't care.

***

Sarah was nothing if not logical so… first came the bath, next came the physical.

Sarah sat in her local veterinarian's waiting room with Charlie.

A woman vet tech called, "Sarah?"

"Right here."

"Room one's open."

Sarah took Charlie into room one and the vet tech took him to get weighed and brought him back moments later.

"There we go. Your guy weighs fifty-five pounds."

"He's a Labrador, right?" Sarah asked.

"Looks like it. The doctor will fill you in."

A moment later the vet came into exam room one.

"Hello, I'm Brendon Wilson," he said, offering his hand. "And who's this handsome guy?"

"Hi Doctor Wilson, I'm Sarah Watson, and this is Charlie. I found him yesterday and I'm keeping him."

Dr. Wilson scratched behind Sylvester's ears and Sylvester wagged his tail so hard his butt was vibrating. "He's a sweet boy," Dr. Wilson complimented her. "Nice disposition. Typical for a Labrador Retriever."

The vet gave him a once over then gave Sarah the news.

"He's been well cared for and he's healthy, but we scanned him for a chip and he has one."

"What does that mean?"

"He has a microchip, Sarah. He's lost. Somebody owns him. Our vet tech's checking with his owner now."

Sarah found that she was literally shaking. She sat down with a thud on one of the chairs in the exam room. "I can't lose you today, Charlie," she whispered when the vet left the room for a moment.

Dr. Wilson came back into the room with a manila folder and smiled. "It's your lucky day, Sarah! You're all set. The lady said you can keep the dog. She gave me her number so you can call her back."

Sarah's eyes lit up. "Really?"

Wilson did his best Shrek impression. "Really, really!" he laughed.

Sarah stopped at the receptionist's desk, paid the bill, and she and Charlie headed for the car. Once inside, Sarah found herself sobbing with relief. Charlie whimpered with worry and kept nosing her cheek with concern.

"I'm OK, buddy. I'm OK. Both of us are OK. It's you and me against the world, Charlie. We're a team now."

***

Sarah made a sandwich and a half from a fresh order of deli turkey. "You want mayonnaise with yours?" She asked Charlie.

"Wuff."

"How about some potato chips?"

"Wuff, wuff." He was bouncing enthusiastically, and his tail was wagging furiously.

"OK, I'll take that as a yes. You don't get wine with your sandwich, though. You're too short." She grabbed a jar from the refrigerator and twisted it open. "I'm pretty sure you don't need dill pickles either," she commented as she fished a couple dill spears out, added them to her plate and put the jar back in the fridge.

While she still had the refrigerator door open, she grabbed a chilled, nearly full bottle of pinot grigio, and added it to a small tray sitting on the counter.

"Whoops, almost forgot," she caught herself. Adding a glass to the other items, she plunked a cube of ice in the glass, then grabbed the tray, turned, and headed for the front porch. She was followed closely by a prancing Charlie.

Sarah placed the tray on the small occasional table which sat between a pair of folding aluminum patio chairs on the front porch, set Charlie's paper plate on the floor and sat down herself. Charlie cheerfully inhaled his half sandwich and noisily crunched his chips then looked toward Sarah, hoping for more.

"Forget it. You're a little piglet. These are mine. Go lay down." A disappointed Charlie huffed loudly and dramatically threw himself on the floor.

Sarah sat with Charlie, quietly enjoyed her lunch and a glass of wine, refilled her glass then picked up her phone to call Samantha, Charlie's former owner.

"Hi, this is Sarah Watson, I'm looking for Samantha. I'm the one who found her dog, Charlie."

"Hi, Sarah, I'm Samantha, and his name is actually Sylvester. But Charlie's a nice name, too."

"Where are you located, Samantha?" Sarah asked. "Are you local?"

"I'm in Chapel Hill. My husband and I were having trouble with our marriage, I have to travel a lot for my company, and under the circumstances there was just no way I could care for him. I had another trip coming up and my brother-in-law said he'd drive him to a Labrador rescue group. He told me they'd find a loving home for him. Isn't that where you got him?"

"Nope. Somebody dumped him by the side of the road. I'm down in Apex. How he made it here without being hit by a car I have no idea."

"Jeezus H. Christ!" Samantha said angrily. "That's like twenty-five miles from here! What the actual fuck? That son of a bitch," she said angrily. "I will rip his fucking face off for doing that to Sylvester."

"Well," Sarah said. "He's safe now, and he landed in a loving home. Were you able to work your marriage problems out?" she asked politely.

Samantha snorted. "Turns out my husband decided he's gay, and is sucking dick."

"Holy shit." Sarah refilled her glass.

"Yeah. Wouldn't it have been nice if he'd thought to tell me that before he married me?" she sighed in exasperation.

"Maybe he didn't know?" Sarah ventured.

"Oh he knew. I found out for sure that he did know. I hired an investigator. My parents are wealthy and they're older. My husband and his sleazy trailer park boyfriend decided to set me up so that when my folks died he could divorce me and the two of them would end up with a shitload of money. Did I remember to tell you I was supporting him?"

"Uhhh... I was just calling about Sylvester, so ummm..."

"You gotta hear this... so anyway, what happened was..." Samantha apparently needed to vent, so she just kept on talking for another forty-five minutes. Sarah actually had to run inside to retrieve one of the AA portable battery chargers to make sure she wasn't disconnected.

Three more glasses of wine later, Sarah managed to gracefully get off the phone.

"Well thanks for all the info about Sylvester, Samantha. I've got company coming," she lied. "So I'll need to run. I hope everything works out for you. Take care. Bye."

Sarah took a deep breath and looked over at the dog.

"What a shit show buddy," Sarah shook her head as she threw her arms around him and snuggled the dog. "Total circus. You're lucky to be out of there." His tail wagged happily.

"So listen, as long as we're talking, it seems we have two names for you. So I'll let you choose. Sarah balled up both fists and presented them to the dog. "OK, my left hand is Sylvester, my right hand is Charlie. Pick one."

The dog looked at her and cocked his head. "Go ahead," she urged. "Pick one," she said. "That one is Sylvester, and this one is Charlie." She nodded at each in turn.

He had no clue what he was supposed to do. He just wanted to make her happy. He licked the closest hand.

"And there we go. Sylvester it is. *Sylvester!*" she squealed, and the delighted dog ran in excited circles.

Sarah was happy. Sylvester was ecstatic. She and Sylvester had seriously bonded.

He'd go for a ride with her with his head hanging out the window of the car, he'd walk without a leash and not run away, they'd play catch, and he was, in fact, a blanket hog. But she didn't really mind. She just bought a second blanket.

***

The two of them were lying in bed, contemplating getting up to start the day. Sarah stroked his silky head.

"You saved my life Sylvester. I've really been missing being able to spend time with Ed, but I honestly cannot bear to be around that boob-heavy airhead, Sadie, he's been boffing.

"I swear to God, it's like his brain has been on vacation. I've seen it happen with other guys before, but jeez, this little gold digger is so fucking obvious it's flat out embarrassing."

"You've been keeping me sane, Sylvester. I drink less and with you here, I have responsibility and purpose. But you know what? I think I need a change. I'm going to start considering my professional options. I've got a good education, a decent brain, I work really well with people, and I can do other things besides teaching college.

"I'm going to start looking at openings. If I need to move in order to take advantage of a position, well, you and I can do that too. I think it's time for us to spread our wings Sylvester."

Sarah sat up and swung her legs over the side of the bed. "OK, I have an idea. Suppose you let me grab a shower and the two of us will go for a ride. We'll drive through some nice neighborhoods in Cary to see what appeals to us. Cary's the seventh largest community in the entire state, so there should be plenty of job opportunities. And..." she leaned down and spoke directly to Sylvester, who had promptly bounded out of bed. "There's a good size community college there, so I can always pick up some classes if I don't find the type of job I'm looking for right away."

Sylvester was focused on the word 'ride'. He was up for anything that had to do with going for a ride. His tail was wagging.

Sylvester began barking furiously just as Sarah was almost finished with her shower. She shut the water off, wrapped a towel around herself and glanced out the window that faced Ed's house. She saw flames and smoke coming from Ed's driveway.

"Jesus!" she yelped, ripping off the towel, yanking on a pair of gym shorts and pulling a T-shirt over her head. She shoved her feet in a pair of sandals, grabbed her phone and flew out the door, leaving it wide open. She took off running at top speed toward Ed's place. Sylvester was close on her heels.

Ed was drunk and stumbling, yelling incoherently at the Corvette, which was totally ablaze.

"Get away from the car, Ed, the goddamn thing could explode!" She grabbed his arm and dragged him back, quickly scanning the yard for a hose. Her primary concern was that if the car exploded the house would catch fire. She quickly dialed 911, gave them the address and yelled that a car parked next to the house was on fire. Within seconds she could hear sirens on the way.

"Ed... Ed, pay attention. What happened?"

"My new Corvette is on fire. Goddamn squirrels." He started to approach the car again but stumbled and fell when Sylvester grabbed the loose material on his trousers and yanked him backwards.

What the hell? thought Sarah, as she grabbed him, helped him stand and dragged him away from the flames again. Sylvester stood protectively at her side.

"Don't bother to call anybody. I can put it out by myself!" he insisted.

"Ed, honey, they're already on their way. Why don't you tell me what happened here?"

"Goddamn squirrels. There's no fool like an old fool. Caught her stealing money from me."

"You caught Sadie stealing from you?"

He nodded sadly and a tear ran down his cheek.

"I shoulda known, right? No fool like an old fool."

"Ed... sweetheart, how did your car catch on fire?"

"I threw her ass out, you know. I just called the credit card companies, told 'em I lost my wallet and cancelled all of 'em."

"Ed... *How* did your car catch on fire?"

He just shrugged. "I think she was pissed that I caught her before she had a chance to do any real damage."

"Jesus, Ed...Do you think Sadie set your frigging *car* on fire?"

They heard popping sounds coming from the car. Stumbling, Ed pulled away from Sarah and headed back toward the car. The fire engines and a tanker truck were rolling to a halt, and one of the firemen, seeing Ed heading for the car, ran up, leapt off the truck, grabbed him, spun him around, and marched him away from the flames.

"Not safe, sir. Suppose you watch the action from over here with your daughter and let us take care of this for you."

"Goddamn squirrels," Ed announced again.

The fireman gave Sarah a questioning glance.

"Squirrels?"

"Beats the hell outta' me," she told him.

"Keep your dad over here with you, OK?"

Ed nodded. "I'm gonna stay over here with my daughter," he announced loudly.

And Sarah smiled.

Chapter Seven

New Beginnings and Then Some (Maybe…)

Sarah had given the matter of her career some serious thought, and in the end, common sense had prevailed.

It's illogical to throw away a well-paying position and several years spent with the university if the only thing I really need is a change, she decided. "So, what are my options?" she asked herself.

Suppose I change the course I'm teaching? What would happen if I modified it so that it was truly unique? Could I convince the university to let me do that? she wondered.

To the best of her knowledge there were no other universities currently offering the class she was now contemplating creating. The uniqueness of her class could be a deciding factor for students to choose this university over their other choices. She was an extremely popular and highly rated professor, and there could be multiple advantages to the university to consider the idea.

So now the question now was whether or not she would be able to talk the dean into pitching her idea to the powers that be, convincing them to grant her a year's paid sabbatical. She thought a year would give her sufficient time to do the final hands-on research.

She wasn't yet certain what NCSU's program was for sabbatical requests. From what she'd seen with other universities however, in general, a sabbatical leave would be granted to the eligible faculty member, for the usual teaching terms of one academic year, at three quarters of annual base salary, plus uninterrupted continuation of existing benefits.

Provided that they agreed with her idea, of course, and saw the potential to the university, she'd likely also write the textbook. Nothing ventured, nothing gained, she figured.

Her proposal would be to create a course entitled,

<u>Technology, Marketing, and Game Theory in the Arts.</u>

The interaction between technology and the arts, the way in which words and images influence people, and the way their decisions are made. Central to the course are developments in Western art of the new century, with an emphasis on historical and emerging issues in visual arts, audible arts, and literature.

If the university approved her plan, she told the dean when she pitched her idea, she would apply for a position with one of many of the well-respected national marketing agencies, hopefully one with a local presence, so she could learn and observe, while simultaneously getting hands-on experience for additional course material.

I have a Masters in game strategy and decision making, and a doctorate of fine arts in creative writing, she thought to herself. *That alone ought to at least give me a little bit of an edge over most other job applicants.*

Dean Smith had been delighted to report back that Sarah's request had been approved. Even better, whatever she earned with a marketing agency would not be deducted from her sabbatical compensation. Sarah would complete the current semester, finishing up her night classes, and when asked, told Dr. Smith if the university really found itself in a bind, that yes, she'd consider teaching a night class or two.

All systems were 'go'. It was time for Sarah to spread her wings and leave the nest. Literally.

Crap. I'm eventually gonna have to break it to Ed.

Ed's life had pretty much returned to normal after his belated middle-aged crazies episode ended. Sadie had apparently moved on to younger and more generous sugar daddies, and from what Sarah could see from Ed, had simply faded into a somewhat embarrassing memory he'd just as soon forget.

Ed hired a professional house cleaning service, and although it was possible that Sally might have come out of retirement to make occasional service calls, Sarah didn't feel it appropriate to inquire. Besides, Ed's sex life was his own business.

The Corvette was judged to be a total loss. Sarah never found out whether Sadie had been responsible for setting the car on fire and that was another topic that fell into the category of 'let sleeping dogs lie.'

The insurance company reviewed his claim. The Corvette had been brand new; it was free and clear. The fire department incident report mentioned Ed's 'goddamned squirrels' comment, and he was a long-term customer, so they saw no reason to investigate further. They just sent him a hefty cheque. Apparently squirrels actually have been responsible for occasional automobile fires.

Ed bought an elegant, if somewhat sedate new Cadillac with the insurance money.

***

Sarah had settled on the upscale Lochmere neighborhood of Cary, North Carolina. Most of the stores she shopped at were in Cary anyway, the grocery store, the deli, the bookstore and so forth, so it wasn't as if she were moving very far. She did like the neighborhood, though. It was beautiful, the lots were a nice size, and there were mature trees.

One morning she had caught sight of a small, nondescript ad in the rental section of the local paper. It had been placed by the out-of-town representative of an estate. Sarah placed a call. The price was right, she was familiar with the street, so she rented it sight unseen. She placed a deposit via PayPal and added an option to purchase within twelve months to her emailed offer. The amount she'd offered as a purchase price was absurdly low and she was dumbfounded but thrilled when her offer was immediately accepted. Paperwork was completed online.

The home hadn't been occupied for quite some time and had only been used as a vacation getaway home by an older couple. The attorney for the estate told her the place was being cleaned, painted, and fully inspected to make certain anything that needed work would be taken care of before she moved in.

He said there was a local management company that would arrange to get her a key, and if she needed anything to call Beauregard Jones over at BJ Management. She should also remit her monthly rent payment to BJ Management, and she could pay it online on their website if she preferred.

Sarah had swung by Beau Jones' office, retrieved a key, and her very next call as she sat in the car, about to drive away, had been to a locksmith. Mr. Jones had struck her as someone who considered himself God's gift to women, and he'd immediately come on hot and heavy, suggesting they should share a glass of wine and offering to stop by in person to make sure everything was to her approval.

Spare me, she thought to herself.

That evening Sarah and Sylvester were sitting with Ed out by the fire pit. Ed was sipping a rum and coke; Sarah had opted for just plain coke.

It was a companionable silence and a placid Sylvester kept nodding off.

"So, how ya been girl?" Ed asked.

"Busy."

Silence.

Sarah took a deep breath, slipped off a shoe and rubbed Sylvester's tummy with her foot. He groaned happily and rolled over on his back so she could reach all of his tummy.

"I have some news Ed."

"What's up girl?"

Sarah told him about her proposal to the university, about their approval, about her interviews with marketing agencies, what she had thought of each agency and the one she'd finally settled on.

She also explained her logic in deciding to physically relocate as well. Not just the fact that it was time for her to leave the nest, spread her wings and fly, but also her conscious decision to remain near him, which made him smile.

"You grew me up Ed, you taught me about men, money, life, friends, and family."

She began to tear up. "You changed my life. You never abandoned me; you were always there. You became my family, my friend. You believed in me, Ed. You taught me how to get dirty in the game of life but always protect myself. You spent time with me, and you never yelled at me.

"I used to be so afraid you would disappear from my life. I was so broken Ed, but you made me whole. With your guidance, and emotional support, I'm finally at the point where I don't owe anything to anybody, and I've got money in the bank.

"I will always need you in my life Ed. I'm literally only minutes away, so you won't get rid of me that easily. And I can still come over and sit out here with you any day of the week."

"Hell. I knew this day was coming, girl. You're like my daughter Sarah. I'm not thrilled that you're leaving the nest, but I'm comforted by the thought that you'll still be nearby. So tell me about your new house," he invited.

Sarah smiled and enthusiastically gave him the description. "It's in the Lochmere neighborhood of Cary. About ten minutes from here. It was actually a steal, Ed. I was incredibly lucky. It was a terribly underpriced rental to begin with, and it was just on a whim that I presented them with a one-year lease option and they accepted it.

"It's three bedrooms, three and a half baths, plus a small den. It's a two-story, with a fireplace, fenced grassy yard, and mature trees. There's a single car garage attached to the main house, plus get this… a single car detached garage out back with a studio apartment and bath upstairs! I'm not sure yet whether I'm allowed to rent it out or if it's limited to mother-in-law or home office type of use.

"Anyway, the house is a pretty little place and the inside's really nice. Freshly refinished oak floors, new kitchen, brand-new stainless steel appliances, gorgeous countertops, natural wood cabinets and the whole place has been freshly painted inside and out. I think you're really gonna like it when you come see it."

"Is it furnished?" Ed asked her.

Sarah laughed. "No, I'm going to be camping again. But it's OK."

Ed nodded. "Then I'm giving you all the stuff in the cracker house as a house-warming gift. And when I say all, I mean all, including the kitchen stuff. I can't have you inviting me over for dinner without being able to treat me right."

"But Ed, I can't possibly acc…"

"Yeah, you can. Tell me when you're ready and I'll arrange for the guys to rent a good-sized U-Haul truck to move your stuff, so you don't have to deal with a moving company."

A tear trickled down Sarah's cheek. "I love you, Ed."

"I love you too, girl."

***

Sarah had already dropped her month-to-month membership at the gym but since she was in Raleigh anyway, she figured she'd drop by to say hello to Ron.

His back was toward her as he was lifting weights and just as he was setting them down, she playfully called from across the room, "Come on Ron. You can do it. Push, push, push."

He burst out laughing and turned around to face her.

"Hey, stranger. What's up?"

"I'm leaving. Sort of. I'm gonna take a year's sabbatical to design a new university class and write a textbook."

"When? Why?"

"Now. My students need to be kept abreast of what's happening in the world. Things in my field are changing incredibly fast. I want them to be ahead of the curve. Besides, I needed a challenge myself. But I wanted to stop by and say thanks for everything. Everybody well on your end?" she asked.

Ron smiled. "They're all fine, thanks for asking. Oh, and I have a girlfriend now. I think it might be… well… I think it's serious," he said.

"I'm really glad to hear that, Ron. The best of luck to you both. All right sweetie, gotta' go."

He gave her a hug. "Take care," he said.

"You too," she echoed.

***

True to his word, Ed had rented a twenty-six-foot truck with a ramp from U-Haul and instructed two of his handymen, Robert and Duane, to get Sarah's stuff moved. Robert was the designated driver, and Ed had made sure the truck would be equipped with dollies, hand trucks and furniture pads. He had also impressed upon the two of them the importance of making certain Sarah's things arrived clean and undamaged.

Toward that end he had provided both of them with long sleeved white T-shirts and white work gloves. He also promised each of them a $50 bonus plus their regular pay if they did a perfect job. The guys were seriously motivated.

Ed stopped by Sarah's new place during the tail end of the moving process to make sure all was going well, which gave Sarah the opportunity to show him around. He very much liked what he saw and congratulated her on having negotiated an excellent deal. She invited him to stick around after the guys left with the truck.

The home had a spacious wooden deck in the back with wide stairs leading down to the wooded backyard. To Sarah's delight, in the center of the deck there was a lightweight concrete fire pit with natural stone finish and a concealed propane tank. The house had also come equipped with a high quality, built in thirty-six-inch stainless steel gas grill on the deck, and all-weather outdoor furniture.

They enjoyed grilled steak and baked potatoes with sour cream and shared a bottle of wine. Sarah had thought to bring home a couple of raw beef rib bones for Sylvester, so he wouldn't feel left out. It felt like a good way to christen the house.

With Ed there with her, it also felt like home.

***

Sarah had landed a position with Forbes and Michaels, an integrated marketing agency in Raleigh, whose services included PR, advertising, and digital media. The firm's owners had a number of big-name national accounts under their belt, the newest of which was Reed's, a major national clothing company.

When she was hired, Sarah had been told that she would be positioned as a creative and marketing strategist for that prized account. She was also told that the interim account executive had been instructed to get her the file and bring her up to speed. It had been two days and that still hadn't happened, but Sarah figured she'd give it one more day before she raised a flag to the department head. She didn't want to start out her employment by causing problems for whoever it was that hadn't followed through with instructions.

Sarah had been sitting at her desk reviewing proposed marketing campaigns on other accounts she'd been assigned, when a pretty, expensively dressed blonde appeared at her side.

"Hi, you must be Sarah. I'm Shannon Hunt," she introduced herself. "Welcome aboard. Want to have lunch this afternoon?" she invited with a smile. "We generally order in from the sandwich shop downstairs and eat lunch in the break room," she explained. "I'll e-mail the menu to you and stop by to collect you at noon if you'd like. I can introduce you to some of the other folks at the same time."

This feels like a good start, Sarah thought to herself. *Of course,* she cautioned herself. *First impressions have been known to be wrong before.*

Sarah responded positively to the friendly overture.

"Sounds good. Thanks!" Sarah smiled back at Shannon.

When Sarah returned home after work that afternoon, she figured she should probably let her family know that she had moved.

Gawd, every interaction with my family feels debilitating, she thought.

"Here we go," she said to herself, taking a deep breath as she dialed her parents' home.

"Hello?" Pauline answered.

"Hey Mom. It's me, Sarah. Been a while."

"How's your weather?" Pauline inquired. Sarah rolled her eyes.

"Weather's fine. I wanted to let you know that I've moved. I've rented a home in Cary, North Carolina, with an option to purchase, and I took a year's sabbatical from the university to create a new class and write a textbook. I'm finishing up the current semester and if the university finds itself in a bind, I told them I'd consider teaching a night class or two."

Silence.

"And I adopted a dog. A Labrador Retriever. His name is Sylvester."

Silence.

"I'm also working at a marketing agency during the sabbatical as part of my research."

Silence.

"It's about to snow up here," Pauline commented, deliberately ignoring Sarah's news.

"Oh, that should be nice," Sarah responded. "Listen, Mom, I'm sorry but I've gotta run. Tell Dad and Jackie hello. Bye."

"Bye."

Sarah disconnected the call and sat there staring at the phone for ten long seconds.

I swear, I will never get used to this dysfunction, Sarah thought, shaking her head in dismay.

***

Sarah set the phone down and headed to the kitchen to fix dinner for herself and for Sylvester. After dinner she got comfortable on the sofa with her tablet and started making notes on what she wanted to cover in her new textbook.

A couple of hours later she went in for a shower, then pulled on a comfortably oversized T-shirt and panties, and crawled into bed, giving her phone one last look for messages before shutting off the lamp on the nightstand.

There was one new message that had just come in. It was flagged, indicating an important message, and the sender was Shannon. The message alerted her that there would be a five-person meeting in the small conference room regarding the Reed's account the following morning at eight a.m. sharp.

Good, Sarah thought. *That means I can finally get started on that account. Glad I checked messages tonight instead of in the morning,* she thought. *Or I might have missed the meeting.*

Then she frowned. *Wait a minute. It's fucking ten o'clock at night. I wasn't supposed to see this message. There's no other reason why Shannon would have waited five hours after the office closed to alert me about an important meeting scheduled for first thing in the morning. The office normally opens at nine. This meeting is scheduled for eight. That fucking bitch is playing games. I'm being set up. This is sabotage. She wanted me to miss the meeting.*

Sarah scowled. "Now let's think about this logically," she said to herself.

I was supposed to have been given full information plus the agency's file on the Reed's account a full three days ago.

Son-of-a-bitch.

I'll bet Shannon's the one who's got the file and she's trying to screw me out of the account.

Well, this is an interesting lesson. I had no idea that I'd have to add a chapter on self-defense from corporate backstabbing, but I'm sure as hell going to consider adding it now. It seems reasonable to alert my students that their foray into the business world is unlikely to be all lollypops and unicorns.

After giving it a bit of thought, Sarah made a decision. *I think maybe I'll play it cool in the morning, pretend I never got the message, and just happen to show up at the office early.*

Sarah hopped out of bed, padded barefoot to her laptop in the den and turned it on.

"Time for a little homework," she said to herself, and used her university account to log into the otherwise inaccessible information sites she figured she'd need to fight fire with fire.

***

The following morning, Sarah arrived early, and was seated at her own desk, ostensibly working on something else. One of the other three people assigned to that account who were expected to be in the meeting stopped by her desk.

"You coming?" Bill Grant from the art department asked. "Mr. Forbes will be here pretty soon."

"What's going on?" Sarah asked innocently. The coworker looked startled. "Didn't Shannon tell you there's a meeting with Mr. Forbes at eight this morning? He wants an update on what we plan to pitch to Reed's."

"I was just about to check e-mail this morning… let me see…" Sarah made a big display of pulling up her e-mail on her phone. She wanted a witness to this part of her plan.

"Let's see, aha! Here's an e-mail from Shannon flagged as important that says there's an eight a.m. meeting this morning with Mr. Forbes in the small conference room to discuss the Reed's account... annnnd... Oh my goodness! She sent it at ten p.m. last night! I was already asleep by then, and when I was hired, I was told that we opened at nine a.m. Boy, it's a really good thing I just happened to get here early," Sarah looked directly into Bill Grant's eyes, all wide-eyed innocence.

He grinned. "Atta girl. Listen, Shannon's a real backstabbing bitch. And a word to the wise, she'll also steal your ideas and claim them as her own. She's done it to me twice now. By the way, Sarah, just between you and me... I don't know what the real story is, and Forbes *is* married, but I do know Shannon's got him wrapped around her little finger, so forewarned is forearmed."

"Got it," Sarah nodded. "Thanks, Bill."

"C'mon, kid, let's make sure we're in the conference room before Forbes arrives," he encouraged.

Sarah pulled a blank yellow legal pad and a pen from her messenger bag and headed toward the conference room. She didn't want to alert Shannon to what she had in mind, should it be necessary, so she'd slipped her printouts between the pages of the legal pad. For all anyone knew she was just a new hire, ready to take notes at a meeting.

Bill and Sarah were already present when Shannon and the fourth employee, Martin Babcock, arrived.

"Hey, Shannon," Sarah greeted her cheerfully. Shannon looked mildly annoyed to see her there.

"Oh, hello... Sarah," she said, as if she'd forgotten Sarah's name.

John Forbes entered and took the chair at the head of the conference table. Sarah pegged him instantly. He was tall, refined, touch of gray at the temples, expensive suit, somewhat abrupt, no nonsense, and very, very smart. She knew exactly how to deal with this one.

"Good morning, group. I've got a meeting across town at nine-thirty, so let's try to get through this fairly quickly, please," he said.

"I want everybody on the same page for the Reed's account. That's why you're all here this morning. Shannon, you were instructed to give the file to Sarah and bring her up to speed. Is there anything you want to contribute to the discussion before I ask Sarah to present her proposal to us?"

Sarah caught Forbes' eye, raised her hand and said, "I have not received a file, nor have I received any information on the account. I was also not informed who had the file or what information I was to have received. All I knew of the account was what I was told when I was hired. "

Forbes turned and glared at Shannon.

She smiled sweetly at him. "John... uh... Mr. Forbes... I really need to keep this account," she told him. "Giving it to Sarah would simply have been counterproductive and a waste of time, because I've already come up with a marketing plan for this account." She opened a manila folder and gave a brief presentation on what Sarah, had she graded it, would have given a C minus. Forbes, on the other hand, seemed to be OK with it.

He turned to Sarah and proceeded to openly scold her in front of the others.

"Sarah, Sarah, Sarah…" he shook his head disappointedly.

"Yep, that's me, sir."

"I hired you for the Reed's account. I expected great things from you. I gave you a chance."

Out of the corner of her eye she could see Bill Murphy, whose face reflected a feeling of helplessness at being unable to come to her rescue.

"With all due respect, sir," Sarah replied. "I was never given the file and I was also never given any details about the account by Shannon."

Shannon sat silently with a self-satisfied smirk on her face.

"I would have expected you to have taken the bull by the horns to make things happen," Forbes lamented.

"Well of course you would, sir. So naturally that's what I did," Sarah replied matter-of-factly.

Forbes looked startled and Shannon's self-satisfied smirk disappeared.

"You have a proposal for us?" Forbes asked.

Sarah smiled sweetly. "Well, of course, sir."

"Although Shannon's proposal was certainly… adequate," Sarah began. "It struck me as being something which might have come from a less… sophisticated firm, certainly not something one would have expected to see from a firm the caliber of Forbes and Michaels.

"First of all, Reed's is not simply a 'clothing company'." Sarah used air-quotes with that term. "Which is the way the foregoing proposal presented it. Reed's produces private labels for major retailers…"

Forbes interrupted her, "Examples?"

"Bloomingdales, Nordstrom, Dillard's, Lord and Taylor, Macy's… although Macy's is in the process of closing a number of stores…"

"Continue," Forbes instructed, cutting short her recitation of stores Reed's manufactured for.

"Reed's also has their own lifestyle brands, which they create from scratch and market online. Reed's is physically located in one of the top six garment districts in the nation. In addition to factories in the U.S. they work with the premiere foreign garment factories on the planet.

"Their reputation is of utmost importance to them, so is consistent quality. Their reps do onsite inspections of the foreign factories they work with on a regular basis. They cannot take a chance on negative publicity. For example, someone suggesting that they use child labor, or that the factories they use pay sweatshop wages, or intimating that the quality of the fabric they employ is in any way substandard, would be an anathema to them.

Forbes interrupted her, "From what country are most foreign manufactured garments sourced?"

"Using the World Integrated Trade Solution calculator and 2016 numbers, China is at the top of the list, although China has slipped about 14% over the past few years. They export roughly a hundred ninety-one million dollars' worth of clothes annually. Next on the list is Bangladesh, at near thirty-four million, so as you can see, China is really the elephant in the room. Fourteen percent won't hurt them at all, but it will stir competition amongst the other nations."

"Where do US garment exports stand on that list?" Forbes asked curiously.

"The US is at number eight, we export roughly twenty million, three hundred thirty-five thousand dollars' worth of clothing," she replied.

He nodded. "Proceed."

"Reed's is interested in getting the biggest bang from their marketing buck. They also want to add a particularly unique lifestyle brand and coming up with both a name and logo will be part of our assignment."

"What's the name you're proposing?" Forbes demanded.

"It's pronounced SEE-nay, and I'm currently working with Bill here on the artwork for the logo."

"How do you propose giving them 'the biggest bang for their buck'?" Forbes quizzed Sarah.

"Cooperative advertising, sir."

Forbes raised his eyebrows appreciatively. "Very good. Nice work. Sarah, keep me in the loop, and Bill, show me the logo when you have it. All right people," he glanced at his watch. "I've gotta get going."

"Shannon, give Sarah your file and tomorrow I want you to take her over to the local branch of Reed's and introduce her."

Forbes hurried out of the room followed by Shannon who departed in a huff, looking well and truly pissed.

The fourth employee, Martin Babcock, softly quipped on his way out the door, "Nice fireworks display. And it wasn't even the fourth." This prompted a grin from Bill.

Bill leaned in and quietly asked, "You gonna show me what the logo I'm supposed to already working on looks like?" he joked.

She handed him a printout of her logo design. "Nice. *very* nice," he complimented her. "What color do you want it to be?" he asked.

"We're shooting for upscale, so I'm thinking metallic gold," she told him. "What are your thoughts?"

"Yeah. I agree. Gold it is."

Sarah stopped and picked up a couple bottles of wine, a pound of cooked shrimp, a head of lettuce and a cellophane bag of fresh tomatoes on the vine, on her way home.

As she drove, she gave a voice command to her phone. "Call Ed."

"Hey girl," he answered happily.

"You got plans for dinner?" she asked.

"Nope."

"I'm on my way home. Think you could handle a fresh shrimp salad and a bottle of chilled pinot grigio at my house?"

"I'll be on my way in ten minutes," he laughed. "Need anything?"

"Only you," she smiled.

Sarah pulled into her driveway and was somewhat less than thrilled to see Beauregard Jones from BJ Management there. There was also a weathered pickup truck parked in front of the house.

Jones was standing over a laborer who was industriously tearing out a section of grass under the oak tree in the front yard.

Shit. Now what?

She got out of the car and walked over to Jones.

"Hello, Mr. Jones. Ummm… To what do I owe the pleasure of your company, and what exactly is it that's going on in my front yard?"

"Hello Sarah. I'm making arrangements to have a metered sprinkler system installed, and I thought that first that I'd have Jose here put a flower garden in for you. You're going to like it."

"Mr. Jones, first, please call and ask for my permission, instead of simply showing up unannounced. Also, unless I specifically ask for something like that to be done, I do not want you to make any changes. I definitely do not wish to incur the expense of a metered sprinkler system at this point in time, and had I wanted a flower bed in the front yard I'd have preferred to specify the location, as well as the content of the garden myself."

"Well, Sarah," Beauregard Jones said condescendingly. "I'm the property manager, so it's my job to make certain the home always looks its best. You're not being charged for this, I'll be billing the owner for it. Besides, according to my notes you only signed a year's lease, so once that's up I'll be putting the house on the market and..."

"No," she interrupted him.

"No," she repeated quietly but firmly. "You will not."

"Excuse me?" he said.

"You will not be putting this home on the market," she repeated.

"But that's part of my job," he insisted. "I manage properties. I rent them; I sell them. I work for the owners."

"Good. Please go sell someone else's house. My lease contains a provision, right there in black and white, stating that I have the right of quiet enjoyment. You are preventing that from happening, Mr. Jones."

Sarah turned to the workman. "Jose, you are welcome to finish digging the flower bed, and I will pay for your work. But I must be the one to choose the flowers," she said.

Jose kept his eyes on the ground, but she could see a smile playing around the corner of his mouth. She had the impression he didn't much care for Jones.

"I will want maximum color year-round, but I would prefer to have pastel colors, which means no fire engine reds or reddish oranges please, because they clash with pastels. Tell me your cell phone number and I will send you a text. You will be able to call or text me, tell me what you propose to plant and where you'd like to buy it from.

I'll call them and pay for the purchase. You may also order whatever soil, mulch, or other ground cover you'll need in addition to the plants. May I assume that you have done this before?"

"Many, many times, senora. I do very good work. I will send you photos and references. You will be very happy with my work."

Sarah nodded and keyed Jose's cell phone number into her iPhone as he rattled it off to her.

"I'll send you some of my flower thoughts either tonight or first thing in the morning," she told him.

He smiled. "Sounds good. Then I send you photos of my other work and I finish digging tomorrow, is OK?"

"That's fine."

"Now then," Sarah said. "If you'll excuse me, Mr. Jones, I'm expecting company to join me for dinner. I'll expect you to respect my wishes. Good day and have a pleasant evening."

She wheeled around and headed for the car to unload her groceries.

Sylvester had a slightly undersized dog door, too small for a potential burglar, but big enough for a Labrador to wriggle through. It allowed him the freedom to be inside or outside when Sarah was at work. He was wildly happy to welcome her home and equally delighted to see Ed when he arrived for dinner.

Sylvester positioned himself beneath the little dining room table as Sarah and Ed enjoyed their dinner, and he rolled over so that she could rub his tummy with her bare foot.

    Life was good.

Chapter Eight

Didn't See This Coming (But Should Have)

Shannon had put off taking Sarah to meet with Reed's executives, telling her that representatives from the main office would be in town the following month. She suggested that postponing the presentation would make more sense. That way it could be done in person instead of just showing ideas to the local group and having to rely upon them to boot the plan upstairs for approval.

To Sarah that actually made sense. She remained wary of Shannon, however. Regardless, the extra time gave Sarah the opportunity to arrange to add something unique to her presentation.

By the time the presentation date rolled around Sarah had all her ducks in a row. As planned, she rendezvoused with Shannon in the reception room on the executive floor of the local Reed's.

Sarah wore a simple but elegantly tailored navy-blue business suit. It was clearly a fine quality outfit. There was a pencil skirt with a discreet slit, and a matching one-button suit jacket, worn over a sleeveless scoop-neck white silk shell. Her shoes were navy-blue leather heels, slightly shorter than stilettos. For jewelry, Sarah had chosen plain 18k gold hoop earrings, plus a medium-sized vintage 18k yellow gold Rolex wristwatch, its design understated, with a square face and mesh band.

On the lapel of her suit Sarah wore a small gold pin the size of a nickel, that she'd had custom made in silver, and plated in 18k yellow gold to match her good jewelry. She would be using it as a marketing piece, and if necessary, she could remove it and leave it with them.

It was a thin circle and mounted in the center was the new Reed's logo that she would be presenting today. The lapel pin had been a subtle addition to Sarah's outfit. Shannon had overlooked it, considering Sarah's entire outfit plain and uninspiring.

The jewelry designer Sarah had gone to was a very old friend who owned a high-end chain of jewelry stores, one of which was in downtown Raleigh. He also rode a Harley, which is how they'd met. He was a friend of Big Lou's.

Over the years he had shared some interesting lessons in jewelry and precious stones with Sarah. The color difference between natural and synthetic semi-precious stones for example, and of course, diamonds. He had taught Sarah how to spot the subtle differences between natural mined diamonds, Moissanite, CZs, and synthetic diamonds, even before reaching for a jeweler's loupe to confirm that first impression.

As it turned out, Sarah was not only a quick study, but she also had a very good eye for spotting fakes. As a result, he'd issued an open-ended invitation for her to come to work for him.

Shannon had obviously dressed to impress for the morning's meeting. The only thing Sarah could think of was that perhaps Shannon was attempting to project financial success. Two carat stud earrings, flashy diamond face watch, black patent leather stiletto heels, and although her black and white striped dress with matching black patent leather belt looked like a designer piece, to Sarah's mind it was absolutely hideous.

Good Lord, Sarah thought. *Has no one ever explained to this woman that less is more?*

Shannon was at the front desk talking to the receptionist when Sarah arrived.

"*Omg,*" the receptionist was gushing. "Did you just get engaged? Look at the size of that *rock* on your finger!"

Shannon was preening and held out her left hand so the receptionist could get a better look. "He proposed last night. I had him well prepared before he ever proposed, of course. He knew I wouldn't accept anything less than a four-carat flawless. And he considers himself *so* lucky to have me!" she boasted.

Sarah approached the receptionist's desk. "Oh, my goodness, Shannon, congratulations! May I see?" Shannon eagerly thrusts her hand out so Sarah could take a good look.

"Wow!" Sarah complimented. "That stone is absolutely *huge!*"

The receptionist looked at Sarah and back at Shannon, "Do I get an introduction?" she asked curiously. "Oh. Umm... Diana, this is Sarah. She's new. I'm training her."

Okey Dokey, Sarah thought to herself. *So that's how Shannon plans to play it this morning. Good to know.*

A phone buzzed and the receptionist answered. "Yes sir, Shannon Hunt from Forbes and Michaels is here, and she's accompanied by one of the firm's trainees. Yes, sir. I'll send them in."

Shannon looked pleased by the way they had just been announced. Sarah was thoroughly unamused. This would need a very quick fix, or she'd instantly lose control of the situation.

The receptionist inclined her head toward a hallway. "You know the way to the conference room, Shannon. Down the hall, and third door on the right. Oh, and again, your ring is absolutely *gorgeous!*" Shannon couldn't help herself. She held up her hand so that the receptionist could take one last look.

Sarah had been quietly backing away, discretely edging toward the hallway. Once she heard the 'third door on the right', she was already out of sight before Shannon even turned around.

The door to the conference room opened just as Sarah was ready to tap on it to announce her arrival.

"Good morning!" Sarah smiled brightly at the executive who stood there and reached out to shake hands with him. "My name is Sarah Watson. John Forbes personally recruited me to join Forbes and Michaels to replace Shannon, who's going to be getting married. Mr. Forbes sends his regards and his regrets that he was unable to join us, but he had a plane to catch. He's already signed off on the presentation I've created for Reed's, and he believes you will like my work as much as he does."

She had spoken at a voice level which, while not loud, had clearly carried to every person in the room. It took less than twenty seconds for Sarah to get that out and she managed to do it a full ten seconds before Shannon showed up, by which point Sarah was already being introduced to the other executives.

"Shannon! Congratulations! We just heard the good news. When's the happy day? And let us see your ring!"

Ambushed at the door and blindsided by the barrage of congratulations, a distracted Shannon smiled, held up her ring and politely expressed thanks for their kind words. By that point, Sarah had already been shown to the seat Shannon would ordinarily have occupied. Unaware that Sarah had already introduced herself and set the stage, Shannon took a seat and segued into her plan to denigrate Sarah and take control.

"As most of you already know, I'm Shannon Hunt, and to my right is Forbes and Michaels newest hire, Sarah, whom I'm in the process of training. I brought her along today so that she could watch as I presented our proposal for Reed's."

Sarah was aware of the slight eyebrow lifting those comments had engendered amongst Reed's personnel, particularly the women. They immediately had Shannon's number. Her subtle attempt to diminish Sarah's importance, by declining to use her last name, had not been missed, nor had Sarah's diplomatically amused response to the attempted coup.

Sarah had simply chosen to lean back slowly and dramatically in her chair, with a look of politely surprised amusement on her face. She had decided to give Shannon sufficient rope to hang herself, and she was quite certain it was likely to be a memorable hanging.

Shannon opened her trim little leather folder into which she had placed copies of Sarah's abbreviated presentation to John Forbes the day of their meeting. She had also obtained a copy of the logo Sarah had created, but not the one with the name printed underneath.

Those assembled listened carefully to Shannon's presentation and then began to ask her questions. Since Sarah had only provided an abbreviated presentation to John Forbes a month ago in the office of Forbes and Michaels, Shannon hadn't a clue how to answer some of the questions, and Sarah had no intention of volunteering anything she hadn't already planned to. Shannon also had no idea of how any of Sarah's plan would actually work.

"Now I believe you also mentioned cooperative advertising. With whom do you propose we might cooperate on that advertising?"

Shannon was unprepared for this one but decided to wing it.

"Well... we could stage fashion photoshoots with discretely placed cans of Coca-Cola™, for example," she smiled brightly. That earned her a polite but icy nod.

"This is an interesting logo design, Ms. Hunt. And the private label name you propose for our new line, you say you pronounce it SEE-nay?"

"Yes," Shannon said confidently.

"And perhaps you could tell us what that word means and what the design is intended to signify."

"It's simply a free-form design I sketched out, and I also created the word. It's meaningless. I wanted something that sounded exotic," Shannon blithely lied.

"By the way, that's quite a striking dress you're wearing, Shannon," one of the women executives commented.

"Thank you," Shannon smiled.

The executive turned to Sarah. "And if I'm not mistaken, you're wearing a suit by Apropos, are you not, Sarah? Would you mind telling us where you purchased it?"

Sarah smiled. "Apropos is one of Reed's private labels. I purchased it from the Reed's website. I've had an account with your store for several years. Reed's has an enviable reputation for fine quality, accurate sizing, pleasing designs, and reasonable pricing."

"And the proposed product name and logo information I just requested?" the woman executive continued without looking at Shannon. "Perhaps you could tell us... uh... your own... interpretation... of... uh... Shannon's product name and design."

Sarah smiled. "Of course. The word cigne is French for swan, a universal symbol of beauty. The abstract logo design is a swan. In Reed's."

"And the... I'm assuming custom-made, lapel pin that you're wearing?" the executive pressed.

Sarah smiled, removed the pin and slid it across the table to the woman. "We had this made especially for you," Sarah told her. "Our proposal is in fact designed to allow Reed's to participate in cooperative advertising. We already have a large national chain of jewelry stores with a spotless reputation, whose owners stand ready to commit."

"Thank you, Sarah, thank you Shannon," the woman said. "I think everyone here concurs that this is a very appealing plan. We'll discuss Forbes and Michael's proposal at length and let your firm know our decision."

***

After the meeting with Reed's executives Sarah felt pretty good. She was positive they were going to go for it, and she looked forward to hearing from them.

She had summarized the meeting for Mr. Forbes in an e-mail, and carefully phrased everything as 'we' instead of 'me' so as to present herself as a team player for Forbes and Michaels, and not to speak ill of Shannon.

Shannon, on the other hand, submitted her own self-aggrandizing summary to John Forbes.

Bill had gotten wind of it and confidentially passed the information on to Sarah.

Shannon had told Mr. Forbes that 'her' presentation had been extremely popular, and she was certain 'her' proposal would be accepted. She confided that Reed's executives had been particularly pleased with 'her' explanation that the name cigne meant swan in French, a universal symbol of beauty, and that the abstract logo design showed a swan in Reed's, a play on their company name.

Shannon also told him that she'd had a jeweler duplicate the design in the form of a lapel pin which she had thoughtfully left with one of Reed's executives. She told Mr. Forbes that the cooperative advertising would be with a chain of national jewelry stores. In short, Shannon had lied her ass off to take credit for all of Sarah's work.

Shannon had already left for the day and Forbes was out of town by the time Sarah learned what had gone down, so rather than setting her desk on fire, which she concluded might be emotionally satisfying, but otherwise counterproductive, Sarah decided to go home and calmly think through her best course of action from this point.

***

Sarah turned down her street and headed for home. There was a car parked in front of the house. Beauregard Jones again. *Oh, for fuck's sake. What is this asshole doing here again? Was I not perfectly clear the first time?*

Sarah pulled into her driveway, turned the car off and swung the door open. "Count to ten Sarah," she said to herself. "You're already aggravated. Try not to kill this annoying tool."

OK, I can do this, she decided. Then she got out of the car and headed for Jones who was standing in front of the recently installed flower bed.

"Mr. Jones," she said politely but coldly. "To what do I owe this visit?"

"Hello Sarah!" he said jovially. "Just stopping by to check Jose's work. It turned out beautifully. By the way I spoke with the owners, and they told me that your lease contains an option to purchase."

"That's correct, Mr. Jones. And your point?"

"Well, I just wanted to let you know that if you'd like to sell your option, I have a buyer standing by. This house is exactly what he's looking for and I need to schedule an appointment with you to show the interior to him."

"Mr. Jones," Sarah took a deep, steadying breath.

"Mr. Jones, you have exactly sixty seconds to get off this property or I will call the police and tell him you've been stalking me."

Sarah raised her arm to look at her watch. "One. Two. Three…"

"Settle down now," Jones soothed. "I know you'll be interested in his off…"

"Eleven. Twelve. Thirteen. Fourteen…"

"OK maybe this is not a good time. We can talk later."
"Twenty-three. Twenty-four…"
Jones turned and ran for his car.

***

By the following morning, Sarah had concluded that a discussion with Deandra Schilling, the head of human resources was probably in order.

As Sarah was pulling into the parking lot, she saw Ms. Schilling getting out of her car. Sarah pulled closer, tapped her horn, waved, and called out, "Ms. Schilling?"

Ms. Schilling smiled, waved and stepped up to Sarah's driver's window. "Hey, Sarah, how's everything going?"

"Hi, Ms. Schilling. Actually, I've stumbled upon a situation that rather puzzles me a bit, and I'd greatly appreciate your wisdom on how best to handle it. Do you have about fifteen minutes you could spare for me sometime this week?" Sarah asked.

"Of course! I'm afraid my schedule is overflowing today, however. I think I have an opening tomorrow after lunch. Check with my secretary to make sure, then schedule a time and I'll see you then, OK?"

"Great, thanks!" Sarah replied, then waved and searched for a parking spot. She walked briskly inside and stood among several others waiting for an elevator. The cars were comfortably large, and capacity was a dozen people. There were only eight people waiting for this car, so Sarah was understandably startled when a female coworker stepped inside, moved in close and deliberately rammed an elbow into Sarah's side.

She was so taken aback at the physical assault that she maintained her composure and never said a word. The coworker stepped forward to exit on the floor before Sarah's without apologizing.

"Have a great morning," Sarah called to her as the woman stepped off.

What the fuck was that all about? Sarah wondered.

That evening Sarah had decided she was going to try a new recipe. Gorgonzola sauced pasta. She'd always enjoyed Gorgonzola cheese crumbled on salads, so the recipe had sounded wonderful.

She'd stopped off at Publix on the way home to buy a four-ounce tub of Gorgonzola, a pint of heavy cream, a small tub of sliced parmesan cheese, butter, white pepper and a box of linguine. Dinner was literally orgasmic. But apparently that much Gorgonzola was more than her body was able to handle. A food allergy kicked in from the really high tyramine content in the Gorgonzola, and she landed flat on her back in bed with a major migraine.

Owww — owww — ouch!

"Crap. What else could happen today," she whimpered.

She did some fast research, drank lots of water and rode it out. By morning she was definitely feeling better, but she was still not a hundred percent, so she called in sick and rescheduled her appointment with Ms. Schilling.

The following day, Sarah was back at work and once again realized that Shannon was doing her best to sabotage her, this time on a second account to which Sarah had been assigned.

Sarah had put together an exceptionally strong marketing presentation and as the two of them sat in the conference room at Forbes and Michaels along with Mr. Forbes and another two employees discussing the account. Forbes had liked Sarah's presentation.

Shannon interrupted the discussion, "Oh please, this is so elementary. I'm sorry, Mr. Forbes, but Sarah's simply not qualified to handle this account. I'll need to keep it. And you can definitely tell who has not majored in advertising and creative arts," Shannon sniped sarcastically.

Sarah had reached her limit with this bitch.

"Shannon," she said politely but coldly. "I have read every textbook currently being assigned for the entire advertising and creative arts curriculum. I could ace every exam being given in that field blindfolded, which, if memory serves me correctly, I heard you complaining a couple of weeks ago that the class was so hard you barely squeaked by with a C-.

"I also hold a Masters in game strategy and decision making, and a doctorate of fine arts in creative writing. So, I'm... pretty certain... that I know what I'm doing."

Shannon looked slightly startled at this news.

"Sir," Sarah turned to Mr. Forbes. "I gave this presentation to the client and they flat out loved it. They even signed off on it."

Shannon huffed sarcastically. "And they're going to un-sign-off on your participation, Sarah," she announced. "They've agreed that they much prefer for me to handle it."

Sarah was stunned, and she turned to Mr. Forbes. "Sir?"

"Well, Sarah, if the client insists on having Shannon handle the account, naturally the company has to adhere to the client's wishes."

"All right then," Forbes said. "Any other thoughts for the day? No? OK, then. Go get em'." He abruptly stood and walked out the door. The matter had obviously been settled and the meeting was over.

The conference room emptied with Shannon looking triumphant as she marched past Sarah's chair. Sarah remained in place, reached into her pocket and pulled out her phone.

"Hi, this is Sarah Watson. By any chance is Ms. Schilling free for a couple of minutes? Oh great. I'll be right there."

Moments later Sarah tapped lightly on Ms. Schilling's open door.

"Sarah! Come on in, dear."

"Thanks for taking the time to meet with me," Sarah said as she turned and shut the door softly before taking a seat in one of the chairs in front of Ms. Schilling's desk.

"Now tell me, Sarah, you said earlier that you'd run into something you needed some guidance with. How might I be of help?"

"Well, this is a bit awkward for me, Ms. Schilling. I'm being ignored, bullied, and literally taken advantage of. I didn't sign up for this. This is beyond regular office politics. This is Olympic level backstabbing, and I really do need some guidance. I need to know how to navigate Shannon. She is literally claiming to have done work that I personally produced. And this has happened on more than one occasion."

"Well, Sarah, you know everyone seems to like Shannon. And Mr. Forbes in particular seems to be particularly pleased with her work."

Sarah had to bite her tongue to keep from commenting on that one. "I know, but I trust you for guidance."

"Sarah, to be perfectly honest, Shannon really is the fair-haired child around here. My suggestion is to try to keep the peace, avoid conflict, and give your notice for the end of this next quarter. You've done some very good work in an amazingly short time, you've got a nice sized commission cheque coming, and you're entitled to excellent references. There are other agencies where you could excel without having to navigate this personality clash with Shannon."

So that's how it's going to be, Sara thought.

Sarah smiled politely but her mind was going a mile a minute. Perhaps she could turn this to her advantage. "Well, under the circumstances, I definitely understand your logic, Ms. Schilling. So how about this... if you provide me with those 'excellent references' now and postdate them, I'll already have them on hand when I'm ready to make a move. That will help me expedite my plans for a smooth transition. If you'll also make reference to the amount of my commissions in those references, I believe that will also help me tremendously."

"That's certainly unusual but under the circumstances I see no reason why I shouldn't be able to do that for you Sarah, and I really do appreciate your understanding. I'm confident that you can handle this for just a few more weeks. Swing by this afternoon and my secretary will have them for you."

Sarah rose and gave Ms. Schilling a nod of confidence before heading for the door.

That bitch Shannon is more trouble than she's worth, Ms. Schilling thought. *If that asshole Forbes could just keep his goddamned pants zipped, maybe our employees wouldn't be leaving us for our competitors.*

Once Sarah was gone, Ms. Schilling buzzed her secretary. "Sally, please book me a flight and a hotel for a four-day vacation in Phoenix. I really do need to get away from here for a little while."

Sarah was as good as her word to Ms. Schilling. She kept her distance from Shannon, but she continued gathering every scrap of pertinent information she thought she'd need for her textbook and the new course she had planned. She also casually interviewed a number of employees to get a better feel for each of their job descriptions.

She surreptitiously recorded the conversations so as not to make the people she spoke with feel uncomfortable by watching her take notes. North Carolina's wiretapping law is a 'one-party consent' law, so it was perfectly legal for Sarah to record her conversations with another individual, since she herself obviously consented to be recorded, and Sarah was not requesting financial or other confidential company information.

Time passed quickly and work was far less stressful for Sarah without having to deal with Shannon's sabotage, and she was assembling research information far more rapidly than she had originally anticipated. So, there was actually a gold lining to having experienced the aggravation.

Shannon had originally told everyone she planned to stay on at the agency and would return to Forbes and Michaels right after her honeymoon. In the interim, as the date of the wedding drew near, Sarah had noticed that Shannon was paying an inordinate amount of attention to the firm's biggest clients.

The final quarter that Sarah had agreed to work through for Forbes and Michaels, had finally arrived. She'd already received the postdated references from Ms. Schilling many weeks earlier, and to her delight, not only were they glowing, but she had also received sole financial credit for having landed the national accounts commissions Shannon had fraudulently tried to claim as her own. As a result, Sarah's final, automatically deposited paycheck, was going to be a bit bigger than she originally expected.

Sarah had been carefully saving, accumulating a down payment in order to exercise her option to purchase the house at the end of the year. At this point she was doing well enough to decide that she could easily part with $500 to buy a pair of portable air conditioners, one for downstairs, one for the master bedroom upstairs. She'd deal with the expense of adding central air later. For now, this would more than suffice. After all, it was only the two of them, Sarah and Sylvester.

Sarah was on her lunch break and was seated at her desk at Forbes and Michaels. She had portable air conditioners on her screen. She had chosen the model she wanted, and happily, shipping was free, so she was ready to click *buy*. All she was waiting for was the deposit to register in her account. She grabbed her phone and logged onto her bank. Bingo, deposit made.

Wait a minute. She frowned at the total. *I'm missing about $500. Let me think. I was out for a few days, but I have paid sick leave, so that's not it. I'm due $500 for the Terra account. Maybe that's it.*

Sarah grabbed her phone and headed for bookkeeping. She tapped on the door. "Hey, Fred? Can you check something for me please? This is supposed to be my final cheque, but it seems to be about $500 short. Are my numbers in error or are yours?"

"Neither situation is good," he replied. "Let me check for you," he said. "Give me a second."

"Well, that's weird," he remarked. "There's a brand-new note on the file that says this is not your final paycheck, so based on our cutoffs... Oh, oh, oh, I get it. That's a commission. Commissions are paid quarterly, so... that... rolls over and gets applied to your next quarterly commission cheque."

Sarah frowned in confusion. "That doesn't make any sense, Fred. Today's my last day. I turned in my notice a full month ago."

"Yeah, I see that here in the file, but it looks like... somebody reversed Ms. Schilling's acceptance of your letter of resignation... and the date... the date... wait a minute..." Fred shook his head in confusion. "This instruction was implemented yesterday, Sarah, and it was issued by John Forbes himself."

"What the fuck?" Sarah asked him. "Can he *do* that?"

"I've certainly never heard of it. Maybe he just wanted to make sure he'd have a chance to talk to you before you left?"

"Shit," Sarah sighed in aggravation. "Is he here?" she asked.

"Yeah, I think so," Fred said. Softly he suggested, "If I were you, I'd bypass the gatekeeper and head directly for his office."

"Good idea," Sarah agreed.

***

Sarah dodged John Forbes' secretary by waiting until she left her desk to take lunch, then Sarah tapped on his door as she opened it.

"Oh, Sarah, good. I was just about to ask you to come in. We have a problem on our hands. Shannon told us she'd not coming back when she returns from her honeymoon after all, so we really need you to stay on and take over her accounts."

"I see," said Sarah. "So that's why you withheld a portion of my final cheque, the funds I was supposed to have had released to me today?"

"Oh, well, yeah, I needed to make sure you'd stay. Shannon deciding not to stay with Forbes and Michaels came at us right out of left field. I can override that instruction and have bookkeeping release those funds for deposit to your account right now."

"Please pull up a chair," he invited. "Now then…" he began.

"Excuse me, Mr. Forbes…" Sarah said. "Could I get you to call bookkeeping and ask them to do that now please, before we continue our discussion?"

"Oh sure, of course." He picked up the phone and dialed Fred, giving him the instructions. While he was doing that Sarah discretely logged into her bank account on her cell phone, periodically refreshing the page, waiting for the promised deposit to make its appearance.

When he got off the phone, and while Sarah awaited deposit confirmation, to kill time she asked Mr. Forbes for some background on why Shannon had made that decision. "Maybe the decision had something to do with her new fiancé," he said somewhat sadly. "I understand that he's quite well off. Perhaps he wants her to have the freedom to travel with him."

The deposit appeared and Sarah discretely logged out of her bank account…

"Mr. Forbes," Sarah said, seizing the opportunity, "I'm going to ask you to leave a voicemail for your secretary, instructing her not to disturb us for a few minutes, because I'm going to give you some information you're going to need."

He looked puzzled. "Sarah, I know you and Shannon have had some prob…" he began.

Sarah lifted her index finger in a 'wait a minute' sign.

"Listen very carefully. If you pay attention, you might be able to salvage your partnership. And your marriage." Forbes went dead white.

Forbes picked up his phone and instructed his secretary to hold calls.

Sarah leaned back in her chair and clasped her hands together in a thoughtful position. "I'm going to tell you some of what Shannon has done so far and then I'm going to warn you about what I'm quite certain she's about to do next," Sarah said.

Sarah then related the lies Shannon had told and the backstabbing stunts she had pulled, not just on Sarah but on several other members of the company, which had effectively cheated those people out of portions of their annual bonuses.

Sarah had a wealth of information because many of the employees she had interviewed had candidly opened up to her. Sarah had the facts on tape. She had later made notes from the tape to make certain she'd have each of her facts straight when she eventually related the information to Forbes.

"You're hardly the first man to be suckered by a gold digger, John," Sarah had pointedly switched from addressing him formally and segued into a peer-to-peer conversation.

"But having personally watched Shannon in action, I'd also say that blackmail is probably not beyond her." Forbes had an excellent poker face, but Sarah observed a very faint flicker of fear when she mentioned the word blackmail.

"Shannon has a wealthy guy on the line, so she's ready to make a move from her stable of sugar daddies to this guy, who is obviously no fool. He has her pegged.

"Shannon's been flaunting her engagement ring and boasting that she demanded a four-carat flawless, because she's worth it. I'm going to agree with that. Her engagement ring is a fake. It's not a real diamond. She doesn't yet know that.

"I'm pretty sure Shannon's guy is going to hit her with a prenuptial agreement just as she's about to walk down the aisle in front of a lot of people. She's going to be insanely pissed but she won't want the humiliation. I suspect that she'll look at that big four carat rock on her finger and she'll pretend she has no problem with the request and sign it.

"But Shannon is nothing if not self-serving. Either she's been promised a higher paying job by a rival firm if she brings your clients with her, or she's planning to start her own firm by stealing your clients. It appears that Shannon has been downloading and copying every single file in this office, and God only knows what she's told your clients, but I'm certain she's about to put her plan in motion right about now, Sarah warned him.

"All Forbes and Michaels client data are automatically entered in files marked confidential. That's good. Because there are statutes regarding theft of business documents and I'm pretty sure you didn't authorize her to do that."

He mutely shook his head no.

"You're going to need to become an instant expert on The North Carolina Property Protection Act, which went into effect in January of 2016," she told him.

He nodded silently.

"All right. Just so that we're both on the same page here, John, my resignation was final, and I'm leaving the firm with glowing recommendations and every commission that I earned while working here."

He nodded again.

Sarah stood and looked Forbes dead in the eye.

"You have another problem you're going to want to address pretty quickly, John. You've been allowing loyal employees to get screwed over and ripped off by Shannon. As a result, you stand to lose some really talented folks. A lot of them have already turned in their notice. People are pretty demoralized and you're nothing without your people and your reputation.

"I'm afraid that in the long run, having given that miserable bitch free rein is going to cost you more than you ever dreamed of. Call your attorney, John," she reminded him. "Do it right this minute. Time is of the essence. Maybe he can figure out a way to stop her."

And with that Sarah turned and walked out the door.

It was early morning and Sarah sat on the back deck, enjoying the solitude, the sunrise, the birds, and a fresh cup of coffee.

Sylvester had been playing tag with a squirrel and just returned to the deck to sprawl happily at her side.

Sarah pulled the cell phone from the pocket of her robe and glanced at the time. Pauline would be up by now. *May as well get this over with,* Sarah thought. *Although I swear, I don't know why I even bother.*

"Hello?" Pauline answered the incoming call.

"Hey, Mom."

"Oh, hi. How are you?"

"Good. I finished my research at the marketing agency a few weeks ago, and I earned some pretty good commissions while I was at it, but I think I've had my fill of cut-throat corporate America business culture for a while."

"I'm going to continue teaching some night classes at the university but for the most part I'm going to be working from home during the day, concentrating on designing my new class and writing the textbook."

"How's your weather?" Pauline asked.

"Pleasant, gets a little warm in the afternoons, but I have a lot of shade trees so that helps. Also, I bought a couple of portable air conditioners."

"It's still cold here," Pauline commented.

"How's the dog?" Pauline asked.

Well, that's a breakthrough, Sarah thought. *Something other than weather. There's gotta' be a reason for it.*

"Sylvester's awesome. And he's really good company."

"Your sister just bought an AKC champion Labrador. He was really expensive. Sylvester is just a dog, right? He's not worth anything like hers is?"

"He's worth a million bucks to me, Mom. OK, well, good talking to you. Say hello to everyone. Congratulations to Jackie on the champion dog. Gotta go. Bye."

Click.

Sarah sat there, silently staring at the phone then shook her head. *Why do I even bother?*

"All right, what's it gonna be, buddy, I can pour myself another cup of coffee, or I can throw on some clothes, grab your leash, and the two of us can go for a walk around the neighborhood."

"*Woof!*" Sylvester responded affirmatively to the phrase 'go for a walk'.

"OK but do me a favor. Go poop before we leave. I'll wait right here. Go ahead, Sylvester. Hurry up. Go potty!" Sarah pointed to the backyard.

With a backwards glance to make certain Sarah wasn't going to leave without him, Sylvester tore across the lawn, heading for his favorite pooping place near a stand of pine trees and deposited his contribution toward the use of natural fertilizer. Sarah's yard maintenance guys had told her they'd handle the compost system for her. She could deposit food waste in one of the bins and they'd add the grass clippings, leaves, and dog poop. Periodically the composted mixture would end up as fertilizer in the flower bed and around the trees.

The morning walk around the neighborhood with Sylvester after Sarah had her coffee on the deck, eventually became a pleasant routine for Sarah and Sylvester. It gave both the opportunity to meet and interact with neighbors and make new friends.

One of her favorite spots to stop and visit was literally right across the street. Sean Gallagher and his equally handsome partner Kyle Brewer had two dogs, golden retriever littermates. The guys were in their mid-thirties, and they wrote and illustrated a popular graphic novel adventure series for young adults. Graphic novels were simply longer and now mostly digital versions of old-fashioned comic books, they explained.

One morning as Sarah stood chatting with Sean, Sylvester, off his leash this close to home, suddenly caught Sean's attention. Sean watched for a moment then spoke up.

"Sylvester? C'mere for a second, buddy." Sylvester obediently turned and slowly ambled toward Sean who knelt down on one knee and ran his hands all over Sylvester's silky black coat.

"Sarah, sweetie, you need to take Sylvester to the vet this morning."

Sarah's heart literally skipped a beat. Sylvester was her baby.

"When I was in high school, I worked part-time for a veterinarian and I learned to identify signs of potential problems in dogs that were not immediately obvious to their owners. I don't know exactly what it is. There's just something that doesn't look right. Humor me, OK? Don't wait. Take him to the vet this morning."

Sarah immediately pulled her cell phone out of her pocket as she stood there on the street and dialed the vet's office, asking if she could bring Sylvester in for a check-up. She told them what Sean had just said.

Sarah and Sean used the same vet, Brendon Wilson and Sean's reputation preceded him. He generally knew what he was talking about. They told her, "Bring Sylvester in right now."

Using the lift table, Dr. Wilson brought Sylvester up to waist height. He did a complete physical exam, ran blood and urine tests and did some diagnostic imaging. He also told Sarah that he wanted to do an echocardiogram.

"Think of it as a more sophisticated ultrasound," he explained. "I need to see Sylvester's heart, Sarah," he said, responding to the question in her eyes.

The vet tech came in with a tube of gel and shaved a large area of Sylvester's chest, explaining that dog hair doesn't conduct sound waves very well, and neither do ribs, so the transducer would need to be moved around a fair amount.

The room was quiet, and it had now been darkened. Sylvester was perfectly comfortable on the elevated table, and Sarah stood at his side, softly stroking his head.

Dr. Wilson spoke just one word during the entire echocardiogram, and only the vet tech was standing close enough to hear it.

"Shit."

"All right," the Vet said. "We're gonna go ahead and turn the lights back on now," he announced. "Shield Sylvester's eyes from the light for a second, Sarah, just long enough to let his eyes adjust to the brighter room."

Another tech tapped on the door and handed the vet a folder with the results of the other tests they had just run.

This time Sarah was close enough to hear his all but inaudible comment.

"Son-of-a-bitch."

Sarah's knees felt weak. "It's bad?" she asked, her eyes pleading with him to tell her it wasn't.

He drew a deep breath and exhaled a long sigh.

"Yeah, Sarah. It's bad."

"Can you fix it?" she asked, silently praying for a positive answer.

He silently shook his head no. "Our boy here has visceral hemangiosarcoma. Highly malignant. A very fast-moving, very aggressive cancer. It most commonly affects the spleen, the heart, the liver, and the skin. This one went straight for Sylvester's heart, Sarah. When it affects an organ, it's not something you'd even know was there. And there were no exterior skin lesions that might have given us a clue. Typical time between noticing something is wrong and death is two months. In Sylvester's case he probably started the countdown seven, maybe seven and a half weeks ago. There's a huge tumor on his heart, Sarah. It's going to rupture. It's nothing we want your boy to have to go through."

"Is he in pain now?"

"No, Sarah. Not at all. He just feels a little bit tired."

"We'll need to put him to sleep so he won't suffer, right? He won't feel any pain, when you do that, will he?

"He won't feel any pain, Sarah. I promise."

"Do we have to do it right this minute?" Her eyes pleaded for time.

"No," he said. "We don't have to do it right now."

"How long do I have?"

"You don't want to let it go longer than two days, Sarah. And you don't have to bring him in. I'll come to you. It's better to just let him just go to sleep in his own home."

She nodded, grateful at least for that.

"Day after tomorrow? What time?" she asked.

"David, my other vet tech and I will come by after the clinic closes. Around six-thirty."

"And then?"

"We'll take Sylvester back to the clinic with us afterwards. You're going to want him cremated, right? And his ashes returned to you?" She nodded yes to both. "The office will arrange that for you," he said.

"Are you going to be, OK?" he asked gently.

She shook her head. "No," she said sadly. "No. I'm not."

***

Sarah dialed the phone.

Dr. Wilson and his assistant David had just come and gone. He kept his promise. Sylvester's passing had been both peaceful and painless.

Sarah had been sitting on the floor, Sylvester cradled in her arms, his tail gently wagging. His eyes were peaceful as the vet administered the shot, and she watched as the light, that lovely dancing light in his beautiful brown eyes… quietly went out.

The loss of Sylvester, her buddy, her best friend, her baby dog, had been devastating beyond words for Sarah. She was emotionally shattered.

Ed answered on the first ring, "Hey girl, what's up?"

"Ed..." she hiccupped, as she tried to hold back the tears. "Sylvester..."

It took him less than three seconds to realize what had probably happened.

"Come home, baby girl," he suggested. "You can tell me what happened when you get here. Are you in any kind of shape to drive, or shall I come get you?"

"I... drive..." she gasped.

"Pack a little suitcase. You're gonna stay for a few days."

"Come on home, Sarah," he said quietly.

***

Sarah spent close to two weeks at Ed's compound. The guest bedroom had its own private bath. She had no interest in food, but Ed would tap on her closed bedroom door and leave a tray on a little table outside the door anyway. Nothing he left on the tray required her to make a trip to the kitchen to return plates or cups or glasses or utensils. He just used disposables. He'd also remembered to leave her a couple of boxes of tissues, a roll of paper towels, and a folded drawstring trash bag.

Sarah would open the door to find that Ed had thoughtfully left things like an elementary school size carton of orange juice, a bottle of cold water, a can of coke, a little bag of pretzels. There might be a peanut butter and jelly sandwich in a plastic sandwich bag. Another time there might be ham and cheese with mustard on a hard roll and a little package of chips, maybe a small bag of cookies and a carton of milk. It was his way of letting her know she could hibernate in the guest room for as long as she needed, he wouldn't bother her, but he also wouldn't let her starve.

Sarah would climb in a hot bath and soak for a while as she struggled to quell the grief and get her bearings again. The knowledge that emotional support was nearby, that nobody was rushing her, helped enormously.

And then Sarah would sleep. She slept a lot while she was there. Her broken heart needed to heal.

Gradually she was able to come downstairs, wander around the kitchen and have something to eat with Ed. Ready to sit at the breakfast bar with him… and talk.

She was finally ready to talk.

She rambled, and he let her. She found herself telling Ed about the awful Thanksgiving with her workout instructor, Ron's appalling family. They laughed about Ed's cremated chicken on Christmas. Sarah told him about Beauregard Jones of BJ Management and what a nuisance he'd been. Ed knew Beau Jones. When she told Ed about the time Jones had scurried to his car as she was counting to sixty before calling the cops, Ed laughed out loud.

And Ed nearly fell off his chair howling when Sarah told him of *Super Bowl* Sunday with her friend Molly's strange relatives, who apparently believed that the devil had purchased ninety-one commercials to air during the game, and were adamant that God hated the *Budweiser* horses.

Sarah also related her experiences with Shannon at Forbes and Michaels. Sarah explained what she'd done to nail down the Reed's account while she was there, and how Shannon had lied again and again, attempting to claim credit for Sarah's hard work. Ed complimented her on the strategy she'd come up with for the new brand name, and the unique logo which subtly incorporated Reed's company name into the design. He complimented her on the clever idea to have the logo reproduced as a custom-made lapel pin, one she could wear it front and center during the entire presentation, and he loved her idea of cooperative advertising. He grinned mischievously when she told him she'd pegged Shannon's four carat engagement ring as a fake diamond and how it was that she'd learned to tell what it really was. They both wondered how that debacle had finally turned out.

She eventually touched on her conversation with Big Lou, and how she'd casually wondered why her family seemed to hate her. She told Ed what had happened to her when she was seven years old and her sister Jackie had kicked her, causing her to drop the antique vase, which unleashed a vicious verbal and physical assault by her parents. She showed Ed one of the small scars that still remained from the incident.

She'd never told anyone else about that incident.
Ever.

She told Ed about the question Big Lou had posed to her, wondering whether, if she ever learned why her family seemed to hate her, the answer might finally allow her to leave everything behind, and move ahead with her life. Lou had openly wondered if knowing might finally encourage her to quit calling those people. She was still futilely seeking acceptance, which only seemed to invite more emotional abuse.

Curiously, Sarah found herself relating what had happened that night at the biker's party when Lou had unconsciously used the word 'affirmative' and it had stuck in her head, prompting her to wonder about his own past.

All these random memories. She had just shared them.

Sarah couldn't explain why all of this stuff had come pouring out now, as she sat there with Ed. She only realized that by having done so, the enormous weight on her shoulders, the weight she'd struggled to carry alone for all these years, had somehow felt just a little bit lighter.

When Sarah finally returned to her own home, although it definitely wasn't easy to do without Sylvester being there to greet her, she was at least better prepared to deal with the deafening silence.

She stood in her living room and looked around, deciding she'd need to wait a few days before she was ready to gather together his bed and collar and leash and toys, put them in a big plastic bag and tuck them in the closet under the stairs.

Through their big picture window across the street, Sarah's neighbor Sean saw the Vet's van come and go, and he'd heard Sarah's car leave shortly afterwards that same evening. His partner Kyle mentioned that he'd caught sight of Sarah loading a small suitcase in the trunk, so they knew she was safe and had obviously gone to stay with friends or family for a few days. They were both glad that she had. They understood how Sarah felt. Their golden retriever littermates were an integral part of their own little family.

Sean noticed when Sarah's car returned to its normal spot in the driveway and decided to wait until early evening to knock on her door. He and his partner Kyle were very fond of Sarah and had discussed an idea.

It was about seven that evening when Sean knocked on Sarah's front door.

"Sarah, it's me Sean," he called. "Open up sweetie, I have a present for you."

Sarah still lay on the couch in the living room where she had been dozing off and on for most of the day. Sean's knock roused her, but it took a second for her to get her bearings.

"Coming, Sean," she called to him. "Give me a second."

She pulled herself up to a sitting position and shook her head, trying to clear the mental cobwebs away. Then she reached up with both hands and hurriedly tried to put her sleep tousled hair to rights.

Sarah opened the door. "Hey, Sean, come on in."

Sean carefully closed the door behind him when he did. He was wearing a lightweight navy-blue windbreaker that had been zipped up close to his neck and he obviously had something inside the jacket that he was trying to hide. Sarah figured it was probably a care package of wine and munchies.

"Whatcha got in your jacket?" she asked with a faint laugh.

He had one hand beneath whatever it was and with the other he carefully unzipped the jacket.

A somewhat bemused little furry face peeked out at her and loudly asked "Mommm?"

"Oh my God! Oh my God!" Sarah instinctively reached out to lift a gloriously zaftig furball who wrapped her paws around Sarah's neck and flatly refused to be dislodged.

Sarah headed for the couch. "Come. Sit, Sean."

"Oh my God…look at you!" she said to the cat now on her lap, whose front paws were still wrapped around her neck. The overweight tabby still hung on to Sarah for dear life.

"Mommm?" the cat said plaintively.

"Yes sweetheart, Mommy's here," Sarah told the cat as she cradled and stroked the cat's head. "It's all right, honey, you're gonna be OK."

"What in the?" Sarah began, momentarily at a loss for words.

"Somebody dropped her off at the shelter," Sean said. "They were gonna kill her."

"Over my dead body," Sarah muttered.

"She definitely needed you, and I thought perhaps you might need her. By the way, her name is Maxine," Sean told Sarah.

"Maxine?" Sarah giggled, looking directly into the cat's big, expressive amber eyes.

At the sound of her name Maxine rubbed her cheek against Sarah's and began to purr. "Holy cow, listen to that purr! Baby kitty you'd give a motorcycle a run for their money with that rumble. They should have named you Harley!"

Sarah sighed happily and Sean grinned, a thoroughly self-satisfied look on his face. "I've got all of her stuff in a bag at my place, food, litter, litter box. I'm gonna run get it for you. I'll be right back."

He was back in a flash. "I'm also gonna suggest putting the litterbox in the bathroom. And here's a thought; you might want to put an old towel under the box to keep her from tracking grains of litter all over the floor until you have a chance to pick up a little doormat thing for that."

"Stay put," he said. "I'm gonna set up the litter box. Oh, and I'm told that sometimes cats feel a little threatened by a new environment and might need to live in a small room for a couple of days, but if you ask me, Maxine doesn't look like she feels worried about anything." Maxine had given Sarah a quick head-boop then hopped down and was now busily exploring her new home.

"Sylvester's scent is still fresh in your house," Sean observed. "And that doesn't seem to worry her, so I'm guessing she might once have lived with a family who had a dog."

"I did take her by Brendon's clinic and had him take a look at her. He said she's no spring kitten, she's around eight years old, but he also said she's healthy and barring anything unexpected, he thinks she's probably still got a good amount of mileage on her."

"She's not a used car," Sarah laughingly protested.

"But thank you for being so thoughtful, Sean," Sarah said as she stood to see him to the door. She gave him a hug. "Give Kyle a hug from me. Both Maxine and I *really* appreciate what you guys did for us."

After Sean left, Sarah went hunting for Maxine who was still exploring. She'd obviously found the litter box without difficulty, since Sarah noticed a small damp spot in the middle, so that was encouraging. Sarah's next stop was the kitchen, and she took the opportunity to securely latch Sylvester's dog door. Sean had relayed Dr. Wilson's suggestion that Sarah make sure Maxine remained an inside cat.

In one fell swoop he said that would eliminate the problem of fleas, ticks, disease transmission, and the possibility of being hit by a car. Good idea.

Drawn by what sounded like a faint jingle, Sarah wandered back into the living room and observed Maxine merrily batting one of Sylvester's jingle balls around the room.

"So," Sarah observed to the cat. "I see you're settling in. Listen, I'm going to make some dinner. You want something? A saucer of milk? A slice of turkey? A cat cookie? I think Sean brought some."

Apparently, Sarah had captured Maxine's full attention at the word 'milk', because the cat headed for the kitchen at a gallop, skidding to a halt in front of the refrigerator, possibly hoping for some of each.

Sarah unplugged the toaster and removed it from the counter of the bookshelf cabinet. There were plenty of other outlets in the kitchen. "You have any problem jumping up here?" she asked the cat who promptly demonstrated that she did not.

"OK, then," said Sarah, depositing a placemat on the counter and setting up Maxine's dishes. "In that case, this is going to be yours." Maxine appeared quite pleased with the arrangement. She already had a milk mustache.

"All right, let's get this part over with," Sarah sighed as she pulled out her phone. She sat down at the breakfast bar in the kitchen and dialed her parent's number.

"Hello?" Pauline picked up the phone.

"Hey Mom."

"Hello."

"How are you?" Sarah asked.

"Fine. How are you?" Pauline inquired.

"Not so good, Mom. Sylvester was diagnosed with a very aggressive form of cancer and we had to put him down a couple of weeks ago. It near broke my heart."

"Well, now you're free as a bird," Pauline replied.

"Excuse me?" asked a dumbfounded Sarah.

"Now you're free. How's your weather?"

Sarah couldn't help herself. "Are you fucking *serious?*" she asked, totally aghast.

"I have to go now, Sarah."

Click.

Chapter Nine

It's Never Too Late (Never)

Another three months of the New Year had flown by.

During the day Sarah would concentrate on research, planning the new class, and writing the textbook, and at night, she'd teach.

Three times a week, on Monday, Wednesday and Friday, Sarah taught a two-hour class from six to eight p.m. She didn't really mind the night classes. It helped make up for the reduced income she'd receive during her one-year sabbatical.

This particular night class was English 101. *Quite frankly,* Sarah thought. *I could teach this one in my sleep.*

The university had recently announced that even more traditional courses would be migrated to full credit online distance learning. Naturally, class sizes were limited. Sarah figured she'd soon either be standing in front of a camera and a green screen in the university's on-site studio, or she'd have to think about turning the den into an online classroom. Her one-on-one student interaction would soon be carried out via the web, using the latest real-time conference software.

She'd miss the in-person human interaction with her students, she realized.

But it did make sense. NC State already offered a huge number of undergraduate and graduate online and distance education courses in a wide variety of subject areas. And all of those courses carried academic credits to meet NC State degree requirements or could be transferred to other colleges or universities. So, it was logical.

In the meantime, it was business as usual.

Sarah was seated at the desk in the classroom as students began to trickle in, and she'd periodically call out a greeting as a student arrived.

A young freshman, looking totally intimidated, had just wandered in.

"Hello. How are you?" Sarah called, and almost laughed out loud when the poor kid jumped at the sound of her voice.

"I'm a little nervous to be here," he volunteered. "But otherwise I'm good."

She smiled at him. "You'll be OK, trust me. Grab a seat."

The room quickly filled up and the last one in was a tall, nicely built guy wearing aviator style sunglasses and accompanied by a service dog. A German shepherd. He took a seat near the door toward the back of the room.

Sarah stood, walked to the lectern, and welcomed the room full of students.

"Hello, I'm Dr. Sarah Watson. Is everyone in the right class?

"We are English 101, college reading and composition. And whether we like it or not, this is gonna be us for the next several weeks. Our goal in this class is for each of you to develop proficiency in college-level reading and writing, through the application of the principles of rhetoric, and the techniques of critical thinking.

"You don't have to write that down; I'm reading directly from your class syllabus.

"For anyone not yet familiar with the word, a syllabus is basically an outline of the subjects in a course of study or teaching. Our syllabus also explains the rules of the road in this class. While I go over the syllabus with you, we're going to pass around an attendance sheet. Just mark yourself present, please."

She handed the attendance sheet to the girl in the end seat of the front row, saying, "Mark yourself present and pass it to the right."

The girl looked confused.

Sarah paused. "Is there a problem, Miss?"

"Edwards. Ginger Edwards," the girl said.

"Ummm... Professor... do you want me to pass it to your right or my right?" she asked.

Sarah's jaw dropped slightly, and she blinked both eyes slowly.

"Is there anyone sitting to your left, Ginger?" Sarah asked her.

The girl looked to her left. There were no chairs. "Ooh. Sorry. My bad."

"Don't worry about it, Ginger. Everyone has first day jitters," Sarah said and quickly moved on.

"OK. Also, if you're here with another individual, human or otherwise, whose name is not on the attendance sheet, please add that name, and mark him or her present as well."

That earned her an amused smile from the student sitting in back with the service dog.

"All right, then. This class usually runs two hours. We begin at six sharp. Tonight's class will be a little shorter. We're going to go over the syllabus, after which I will dismiss the class, and if you wish, you have my permission to go to your local watering hole and commence whimpering."

***

The class went well, and as the students were leaving and saying their goodbyes, the nice-looking guy in the back with the service dog stepped forward and offered his hand.

She shook his proffered hand and greeted him. "Hello."

"Hi Dr. Watson. I'm Nick Bowman, and this is Flo."

"Nice to meet you, Nick." She looked down. "Nice to meet you too, Flo." Flo's tail wagged happily.

"I'll need to prevail upon you to sign my own attendance sheet, Professor. The good folks at both the VA in Durham and the Wounded Warrior Project like to stay abreast of what I've been up to. I'm still in the process of transitioning from hell back to the real world."

Slightly taken aback, Sarah asked gently, "Are you visually challenged?"

Nick smiled and removed the aviators, placing them on his head.

"No ma'am. I do seem to be light sensitive now, though."

"I'm sorry," Sarah said, embarrassed. "I thought..."

"No big deal. Happens all the time." He handed her the paper.

"Where do I?"

"Sign down there on that line." He pointed to the spot.

Sarah looked at Flo. "She's beautiful. I know people are not allowed to pet working dogs, but I certainly wish I could. What a sweetheart." Flo's tail was wagging happily.

"You'd have to earn my trust first, Professor," Nick said gruffly.

Flo whined softly, edged a step closer to Sarah and looked pleadingly toward her master.

"*No*, Flo," Nick told her.

Sarah took a step back. "I'm so sorry, I didn't mean to..."

Nick slid his aviators back on. "Yeah," he said. "I know that. See ya," he told her as he turned and walked away.

Flo gave Sarah a longing backward glance, then got back to work.

***

The Veterans Administration Hospital in Durham, North Carolina has an excellent PTSD program, and a group of twelve men were sitting in a classroom listening to a man talk about treatment. The man's name was Carl Johnson, and he knew what he was talking about.

Flo lay next to Nick's chair, her chin resting protectively on his right shoe.

"As you men already know, Johnson said, 'trauma-focused psychotherapies are the most highly recommended type of treatment for PTSD.' 'Trauma-focused' means that the treatment focuses on the memory of the traumatic event or its meaning. These treatments use different techniques to help you process your traumatic experience. Some involve visualizing, talking, or thinking about the traumatic memory. Others focus on changing unhelpful beliefs about the trauma.

"Each of you have progressed to a point where you've decided, on your own, to either to begin college or to return to college. That's a very positive step. So... we're here to help.

"You all have your semester course schedules. Are there any problems with scheduling conflicts or anything in general?" As that line of questions and answers continued in the background, Nick, and his buddy Joe Anderson were quietly carrying on their own conversation.

"How's your schedule, man?" Nick asked him.

"Schedule's not bad. This first course is a bitch, though. I have math. I fucking hate math. You got English first, right?" Joe asked. "Did you manage to land in Sarah's class?"

"You mean Dr. Watson's class? Yeah, I did. What, you know her?"

"Had one of her classes a few years ago," Joe said. "Remember... neither you nor I started college right after high school. I took a job to save money for college then decided to enlist to get college paid for under the GI Bill, and you needed to take a few years off to help your old man. He was expanding your family's ranch back then, and ya'll had a bunch of stuff under construction. You were what, twenty-one when you enlisted? I was twenty-eight by the time I got back."

"Anyway, she's cool as hell," Joe continued. "Hot too. You oughta hit that, man."

"Oh yeah, right," Nick scoffed. "What would a fucking yuppie together bitch like her see in a broke-down Marine like me? Look at me, Joe! I'm a goddamn wreck. I tote a fucking dog everywhere I go. And if I didn't have Flo, I'd still be a fucking shut-in."

Flo, having heard her name, cocked her head and looked at Nick.

"No disrespect, Flo. You saved my life, girl." Nick affectionately stroked Flo's head, prompting her tail to wag happily.

"Nick," Joe protested. "You never know until you try. The woman's a class act. So are you, my friend. You were president of our senior class, straight-A student, athletic as hell, terrific actor in school plays, man you had the freakin' world at your fingertips."

"Yeah, and then my fucking world blew up, Joe. I'm not the same guy that I was."

"Bullshit, buddy. We enlisted to fight for our country. We both did. At least that's what the lying bastards told us we were gonna be there doing. Miserable fuckers. But we made it back alive. A lot of guys weren't that lucky." Joe shook his head remorsefully.

"So yeah, you ended up with shitload of dents and dings, and the chassis might rattle a bit these days, but hell, you're still Nick Bowman. And you're one of the good guys. So maybe you're one of the lucky ones. Hey… nothing ventured, nothing gained, pal. It's just a suggestion."

"Ah… Johnson's done," Nick observed. "I gotta run, Joe. Catch you later, man." The two men and Flo rose and headed for the parking lot.

Nick had rented a small furnished townhouse in Durham, North Carolina, not far from the VA where he had undergone a lot of his medical treatment when he returned stateside. In that part of North Carolina, it seemed as if everything was no more than a half-hour from everything else. Both Raleigh and Cary, where Joe lived now, were in Wake County, and the VA was in Durham County, immediately adjacent to Wake.

Nick and his buddy, Joe Anderson had grown up in Wake County, where Nick's parents still owned a large ranch. His folks also owned a lot of well-located vacant land, some of it waterfront, some of it heavily wooded. Nick's parents had sold off some of the acreage after Nick was injured, investing the funds in an annuity for him, which would provide Nick with the ability to live comfortably, and still save, without ever having to touch the principle.

The purely physical injuries Nick suffered had been grave, but he could deal with them.

The TBI, the traumatic brain injury he could deal with as well. That had left him with light sensitivity, loss of balance, and a number of other things he'd simply learned to cope with. His service dog Flo had been a tremendous help.

But PTSD, the post-traumatic stress disorder, was a real bitch. And the nightmares... dear God, the nightmares... reliving that hellish experience over, and over, and over...

All of it had been a fucking nightmare. The medics had grabbed him, slapped an oxygen mask on his face and then they ran like hell with him. First the emergency room of the trauma hospital at Bagram Air Base in Afghanistan to get stabilized, then he was transferred by cargo plane to Ramstein Air Base in Germany for more surgeries at Landstuhl Regional Medical Center, the largest American hospital outside the US. Once they stabilized him yet again, he had been flown back to the US and taken by ambulance from Dover Air Base in Delaware to the Naval Hospital in Bethesda, Maryland where he spent nearly a year. Finally, he found himself closer to home, at the VA in Durham.

Nick slept fitfully. Flo could always tell when the nightmares were coming. She'd crawl into bed with him, alert to the signs, ready to defend him when they came.

In his mind, as he slept, Nick was back in combat.

There had been six men in his unit's Humvee, their high mobility multipurpose wheeled vehicle when it accidentally drove over a concealed improvised explosive device. Their up-armored HMMWV was designed to conduct reconnaissance and security operations as its primary function. Toward that end the vehicle was equipped with additional armor both on the sides and underneath, which was intended to protect the crew from small arms ammunition and mines.

It wasn't enough. The IED blew four of his men to pieces, the fifth man was critical, his intestines had festooned the interior of the Humvee. He lay there screaming until mercifully the screaming abruptly stopped.

Nick had received a traumatic brain injury, and his knees were shattered, rendering him immobile, he had a laundry list of other injuries, he was covered in blood, impossible to tell how much of it was his, and he was fighting to remain conscious, yelling into the radio for help, praying someone would get to them in time.

In his mind he was still lying there yelling for help when Flo awakened him from the nightmare. He was drenched and shaking, but it wasn't blood he was covered in this time, it was ice cold sweat.

Nick opened his eyes and stared at the ceiling, trying to make the mental and emotional transition from that scene of carnage to the safety of his own bedroom.

Flo was gently licking his face and whining with concern.

"I'm OK, Flo, I'm OK," he gasped. Nick automatically reached over to the nightstand for the bottle of water and a vial of pills. Flo, refusing to leave his side, protectively rested her head on his belly.

Nick glanced over at the clock as he returned the prescription bottle and water to the nightstand. It was three in the morning. He sighed heavily.

Jeezus. How did I get here? My life used to make sense. I used to have a future. I don't know how to deal with any of this shit any more.

Nick shut his eyes.

Flo raised her head and carefully crept forward to gently lick the salty tears away.

***

It was that time again. Sarah waited for the classroom to fill up. She had noted with amusement that on the prior attendance sheet the name Flo Bowman had been added next to Nick Bowman's name.

When Nick and Flo Bowman arrived for this class, he removed his aviators and made eye contact with Sarah for a good twenty seconds before slipping them back on.

She instinctively smiled at him, and her mind wandered for a moment. *Nice looking guy,* she thought. *Looks to be in his early thirties, maybe six foot two inches, alpha male attitude, he's not using a cane and he seems to have good use of both hands, so I'm not sure what the service dog is for.*

She shook herself out of her reverie.

"Miss Edwards!" Sarah greeted Ginger Edwards. "How are you doing today?"

Ginger Edwards laughed. "I'm good Professor."

"In that case I'll hand you this stack of papers and ask you to take one and pass the rest along in whatever direction seems logical." The class was full now.

"Everybody take one please," Sarah called out. "You find a short essay on one side of the paper and a note telling you our three goals. I want you to read it and on the back of that sheet, along with printing your name on top, I want you to tell me three things; one — what you think the author is saying, two — what insight you feel the essay imparts, if any, and three — your honest opinion of the essay.

"Everybody got a copy? OK, good. You have thirty minutes. Begin."

Sarah zoned out during the half hour she gave her students to read the essay and write their commentary. She let her vision roam around the room, studying each student in turn, referring to her notes about individual students as she did so.

When she came to Nick she paused. She made eye contact with Flo and couldn't help but grin when Flo's tail began wagging.

At the sound of Flo's tail slapping enthusiastically on the floor, Nick looked left and right, and seeing nothing, glanced at Flo. He saw she was looking directly at Sarah and that Sarah was grinning at the dog. He smiled briefly in amusement, then went back to his critique of the essay.

Sarah glanced at her watch. "Five minutes left people," she called out.

Then… "Time's up. OK, let's discuss the essay and your personal interpretation. Remember there is no right or wrong answer in all this. Critical thinking is the key my friends."

There was a hand in the air. Sarah looked at her roster. James Brooks. Her notes indicated that he was young and experienced mild autism.

"James Brooks?" Sarah called out. "Would you like to tell us your thoughts?"

"I think this is about a man who had a psychotic episode, left his family, and job and went to find himself. In my opinion, he sold out. He's weak."

"Wow, OK James."

"Let's see, who's next?" Another hand was in the air. "Jessica… Haversham. Jessica, what are your thoughts on the essay?"

"I totally disagree with James. I believe that the deeper meaning is not psychotic but rather a spiritual growth, an evolution of his soul. Tragedy often breeds beauty, peace, and serenity. To disregard this man as selling out is nothing more than a projection of your own soul James," Jessica sniped.

"Keep it civil, people," Sarah cautioned. "Different people see things in different ways."

Sarah called on another ten people.

"Interesting and thought-provoking viewpoints. I look forward to reading the rest of your assessments. Pass your essays forward please. Great job today people. In our next class we'll be watching a short film and breaking into discussion groups. In the meantime, have a good evening."

Sarah returned to her desk with the pile of essays and was in the process of loading them into her messenger bag for review later that evening. Only Nick, Flo, and young James Brooks still remained, and James was approaching her desk.

"Professor?"

"Yes, James. How may I help you?"

"The way you interpreted that essay is incorrect. You need to learn the right interpretation in order to do your job."

Sarah sighed and remembered her notes on this student.

"How old are you, James?"

"Dual-enrollment, Professor, I'm seventeen."

"All right. Now let me explain this to you, James. You are in high school and you're very bright, which is good. But I am not only older than you, I am much smarter than you, which is why I am the teacher and you are not. Now when you come up to me, especially when other people are present, and say something like this, you are insulting me, and that is not acceptable."

"I don't understand. There's nobody here."

"Look around you, James. Do you see someone else in the room?"

"Oh. Yes, Ma'am."

"So we are not alone, are we?"

"No, Ma'am."

"Now James," Sarah explained gently. "I always respect questioning authority, but it's important to understand when and where it can be done politely, and when and where it's not appropriate.

"The correct place for you to have this kind of discussion with me is in my office. And the correct time, is when you make an appointment with me to do so.

"Do you understand that James?"

"Yes, Ma'am."

"All right. You have a real good evening James."

"Thank you, Professor, you too," James said, and with that he turned and left.

Nick had watched the entire exchange from his seat in the back of the room. He rose and approached Sarah's desk with a look of bemusement on his face.

"What... what did I just witness here? How did you keep from smacking that smartass kid upside the head?"

"James has autism, Nick. A mild case to be certain, and although he's really very bright, his brain has difficulty processing some things. He doesn't understand subtlety, or sarcasm, for instance. He also doesn't understand what's appropriate or inappropriate unless it's explained very simply and very directly."

He studied her for a moment.

"Would you... be... insulted or offended... if I offered to buy you a drink?" he asked hesitantly.

"That depends," she replied.

He was slightly taken aback by her answer. "Depends on what?" he asked.

"Can I pet your dog?" she asked. "I think she's been flirting with me."

He burst out laughing. "Yeah, you can. She's a pretty good judge of character."

"You want to ride with me or follow me in your car?" he asked.

"I'll follow you. Where would you like to go?"

"There's a friendly little place in downtown Cary called Sidebar. It's on East Chatham, only about fifteen minutes from here, maybe less at this time of night. They have seating inside and a covered patio outside and it's a nice night, so I thought maybe we could sit outside."

"I know where Sidebar is. I live in Cary," she told him.

"Then we'll walk you to your car," he said.

"I'll drive you and Flo to yours," she replied.

He smiled. "Deal."

The weather was mild and clear, so they did choose a table outside. Nick ordered a beer, Sarah requested a glass of white wine, and without being asked, the waitress brought Flo a bowl of water.

They were quietly and casually getting to know each other.

"Why are you teaching night classes?" Nick asked curiously.

"I have no life?" Sarah questioned with a laugh. "No actually, I'm on a year's sabbatical from the university. I'm designing a new course and writing a textbook. They were short an instructor for this class and asked if I'd be willing to take it. I said sure."

"What about you?" she asked.

"Marine. I'm from here in Wake County, a bit north of Raleigh. I was one of six men in a Humvee that hit an IED during my fourth tour in Afghanistan."

"Damage report?" Sarah asked, point blank.

"All six lost their lives. I just happened to continue breathing."

The finality of his statement shook Sarah to her core. Jeezus.

"You planning on staying dead?" she asked.

Her question startled him. It certainly hadn't been what he thought she might say. So, for the very first time, he actually considered the matter.

"There is no right or wrong answer here, is there, Professor? You're asking because you're interested in what my real thoughts are, right?"

She nodded silently.

"I don't know. I guess the fact that I decided without urging to enroll in a course at the university, indicates that subconsciously, at least, I want to live."

"But obviously there are some extenuating circumstances," he added.

He responded to Sarah's raised eyebrows, wordlessly inviting him to proceed.

"The PTSD is a problem," he explained. "The nightmares are a problem, all the pills I have to take are a problem, the intermittent dizziness is a problem, my forgetfulness is a problem, my flashbacks are a problem, my knees suddenly giving out is a problem, the traumatic brain injury is a problem, the migraines are a problem, the remaining shrapnel is a problem, the difficulty transitioning back to the real world is a problem, I sit in the dark on the fourth of July, and I have shit lodged in my brain. Oh yeah, and although I can have sex, I can only do it if I'm on the bottom," he said flatly.

Sarah silently studied him for about sixty seconds.

"But other than that you're, OK?" she asked calmly.

He shouted with laughter.

"Yeah, Professor. Other than that, I'm OK."

"So, tell me about your family. Are you an only child?" she asked.

He shook his head no. "I have four siblings. All married. Got a bunch of nieces and nephews. Rug Rats. My parents are about a half-hour north of Raleigh. They live on a ranch out in the country. I love the daylights out of all of them, but I haven't really been able to deal with spending time with any of them for a long time now. I don't want to have to see pity in their eyes.

"Before… my last tour, before I got… hurt… I was active. I did everything. I spent a lot of my life on the back of either a horse or a Harley. I used to fish, hunt, skydive, I had a private pilot's license… I had… I had a life."

"What about you?" he asked.

"The opposite of you," she said simply.

"So… now that you know all the problems I come with, what do you plan to do with me, Professor?" he joked.

"Honestly? I was thinking about taking the both of you home with me and introducing you to Maxine."

"Who's Maxine?" Nick asked hesitantly.

"My cat."

***

Nick pulled his Kia Telluride into the driveway and parked behind Sarah's Civic. He stood for a moment when he got out of his SUV, looking around the neighborhood and at Sarah's house. She walked back and joined him. He nodded his approval.

"Nice neighborhood, friendly feel to it. Pretty house. It suits you, Sarah. You have good taste."

"Thank you," she smiled. "I have a lease with an option to purchase that I plan to exercise before the end of the year. Come on in. I'll show you the rest of it."

"Can I offer you something?" she asked, after the brief tour. "Beer? Wine? Cookies and milk?"

"You have cookies and milk?" he asked with interest.

"Yeah, as a matter of fact I do," she laughed. "Glasses are in that cabinet…" She pointed. "Cookies are in the cookie jar on the counter, plates are over there, and there's a gallon of ice cold milk in the fridge. Help yourself!"

Sarah was going through a plastic bag in the closet under the stairs and emerged triumphant with Sylvester's stainless steel food and water bowl.

She put one of the pet placemats on the floor and filled the water bowl. Seeing the dog bowls, Nick looked around curiously. "Where's your dog?" he asked.

"Sylvester's ashes are in the flower bed out front. He had cancer. Fast-moving, and extremely aggressive. There was nothing I could do but let him know he was dearly loved and make certain he didn't suffer. It's been three months now. I miss my boy terribly. He was a black Lab, smart as a whip and intensely loyal. He was also my best friend." She sighed and shrugged. "It is what it is."

"Shall we put some dog food down for Flo?" she asked Nick.

Nick nodded. "She's already had her dinner, but it wouldn't hurt to put a little bit of food down for her," he said. At the sound of the spoon on Sylvester's dish Maxine promptly made her appearance and went face first into the dog food.

Flo gazed at the cat with a slightly puzzled expression on her face. She looked back and forth from Nick to Sarah seeking instructions, and when none were forthcoming, Flo simply nosed in next to Maxine and claimed her share of the food.

"It appears we have détente," Nick laughed.

Sarah leaned over and snagged a cookie from his plate. "Mmmm," she said happily.

"Do you and Flo plan to spend the night?" she asked casually.

Slightly bemused by her directness, Nick asked, "Are we invited?"

"Gotta start somewhere," she replied.

"In that case, I think I can speak for both of us. Yes please, we'd like to stay."

"You mentioned that you're on a number of medications. Do you have an emergency supply that you carry with you?"

"Actually, I do," he replied. "In my wallet."

"Is there anything we should have in the bedroom that you would normally reach for if you had a problem?"

"Bottle of water?"

"Done."

"Day-yum, woman, nothing fazes you. You just survey the landscape and then roll with it."

"You ever do this before?" he asked.

"Nope. Shall I let Flo out to go potty before we go upstairs? Backyard's fenced."

"Yes, please."

"OK. Master bedroom's upstairs. I'll meet you in the shower."

***

On her way upstairs the night before, Sarah had first retrieved Sylvester's bed from the closet and carried it up with her, placing it on the floor in the corner of the bedroom. That was the first thing that met her eyes this morning when she awakened in Nick's arms.

She couldn't help but smile. Flo was curled up in Sylvester's old bed, still sound asleep, and Maxine was comfortably nestled between Flo's paws.

Peaceable kingdom, she thought. She closed her eyes and fell back asleep.

Sarah awakened a second time when Flo was nudging Nick's arm to get him to wake up. He grabbed Sarah and pulled her close, affectionately nuzzling her neck.

"Woof!" Flo reminded him that she needed to go out.

"Stay put," Sarah told Nick. "I'll let her out and put a pot of coffee on."

She rolled out of bed, pulled a robe out of the closet and slipped it on. "C'mon baby dog, wanna go out?"

Flo promptly made a beeline down the stairs, heading for the back door. Sarah was close on her heels and opened the door to let her out.

Sarah put a pot of coffee on to brew, pulled a pair of mugs down from the cupboard, then set creamer, sugar, and a couple of spoons on the counter next to the now fragrantly brewing coffee maker.

Maxine was next downstairs, loudly insisting that it was time for her breakfast. Sarah prepared the dishes for both the cat and the dog, then let Flo back in when she heard a quiet wuff at the door.

Flo didn't stop to eat though, instead she galloped upstairs to check on Nick.

Within a moment or two, Sarah could hear Nick moving around upstairs so she slipped Maxine's halter and leash on, then unlatched the dog door so Flo could have breakfast then go back outside if she wished.

Sarah then fixed her own coffee, slipped on the pair of sandals she kept by the back door and left a note on the counter for Nick, saying,

'We're on the back deck. Grab coffee and join us. Cereal is in the cupboard, bagels and cream cheese are in the fridge. So are bacon and eggs. Have anything for breakfast that you'd like.'

Sarah and Maxine headed for the back deck. Maxine's leash clipped onto to a long lightweight lead which allowed the cat to wander about the deck at will without getting too close to the edge. Sarah flicked the fire pit on to take the edge off the morning chill, then leaned back in the comfortable chair and peacefully savored her mug of coffee.

After a few minutes, Sarah could hear Nick rattling around in the kitchen. A little while later, he joined her on the deck, a toasted bagel with cream cheese and a light sprinkling of kosher salt on a plate in one hand, a cup of coffee in the other. Flo had finished her kibbles and zipped through the dog door a moment later, happily settling herself by Nick's chair. Maxine promptly cozied up to Flo.

"I feel like I've been with you forever," Nick said wonderingly.

He shook his head in confusion. "I sure as hell don't understand it, but I like it."

Sarah smiled in quiet contentment.

"I've got appointments in Durham this afternoon and again tomorrow morning," he said, almost apologetically.

"I have your class on Friday…" he ventured hopefully.

"You and Flo are welcome to come and spend the weekend," she offered casually. "Maxine enjoys having a playmate."

He couldn't resist. "Does Sarah enjoy having a playmate?" he teased.

"That depends."

That stopped him again.

"Depends on what?" he asked hesitantly.

"You planning on staying dead?" she asked him for the second time in twenty-four hours.

He silently contemplated the question.

"There *is* a right and wrong answer this time, isn't there?" he asked.

"Yep."

He rose and leaned down to kiss the top of her head. "We'll see you in class on Friday," he said softly.

***

Sarah sat comfortably on the sofa in the living room, Maxine was firmly ensconced on her lap.

"You comfortable?" Sarah asked the cat with a laugh. Maxine just opened one eye and settled herself a little more comfortably.

"Well..." she said to herself, "Suppose we get an expert opinion."

She was calling Frank Marston, another one of the people she'd been introduced to by Big Lou. A weekend biker these days, Frank was a former Marine who'd gotten pretty well shot up in Iraq but who had put his life back together. He now owned a private security company.

The call was picked up but for five seconds the only sound she could hear was a massive barrage of gunfire.

Finally, there was a voice.

"Yo? Sarah, sugar, what are you up to pretty lady?"

"Holy shit, Frank. You in a firefight or what?"

He laughed. "Nah, I'm at the range with a couple of other assholes."

She heard another male voice in the background, demanding, "What's going on?"

"Fuck you," Frank shouted back to the heckler. "I still have ten minutes left."

"Want me to call you back another time?" Sarah asked.

"Nah, go ahead."

"I met someone, Frank. It hit me like a ton of bricks. The thing is, I'm not sure I'm qualified."

"Tell me," he said.

"Former Marine. Got blown up in Afghanistan. He's got a service dog. Takes medications. Can only fuck while on his back. When I asked him what happened, and I'm quoting him verbatim, Frank, he said, 'I was one of six men in a Humvee that hit an IED during my fourth tour in Afghanistan. All six lost their lives. I just happened to continue breathing.'"

"Jeezus. Yeah. I've been there, Sarah. It's not a good place."

Frank was silent for a moment. "Wish I'd had a service dog back then. Might a helped. Took twelve years before I let anybody get close to me again."

"I feel a real connection with this guy, Frank, but this is all new territory for me."

"I get it. The thing is, you have to remember not to lose yourself in this, kiddo."

"What does that even mean?"

"You're a good person, Sarah. You're in my inner circle. If he opens up, the two of you can move mountains. You need to gain his trust. But if he's not ready, you can't force it, and you need to know enough to walk away."

Sarah sighed. "I hear ya, Frank."

A moment passed and she sighed again. "Walking away is not exactly a strong suit for me."

"Then let me give you some advice," Frank offered. "Treat your guy the same way you'd treat a dog that's been really badly mistreated. It's probably gonna take him some time. Don't spook him. Let him learn to trust you at his own pace. Once he trusts you, he'll trust you forever."

A voice in the background was yelling, "C'mon, Frank, get your ass back over here."

"I gotta go, kiddo," Frank said. "Love ya sweetheart."

"Love you too. Thanks, Frank."

Sarah set the phone down and absentmindedly stroked Maxine's head. "I don't know how strong I am, Maxine."

Chapter Ten

We All Have a Past (Embrace it)

Nick sat next to Joe and a mutual friend, Mark Kepler, in their PTSD support group. The lecturer was talking about relationships.

"Only relationship I got is with Rosie Palm and her five sisters," Mark muttered. "It's either Rosie or one of the strippers down at Club TaTa, when somebody wants to pick up a quick fifty, that is."

Nick slapped his head. "Jeezus Mark, do you have a fucking death wish? You mess with that shit and your dick is likely to fall off. Or worse. Don't you read the damn news?"

"Seriously?" a doubtful Mark asked.

"I am *not* kidding, buddy."

"Speaking of relationships, man, did you hit on the hot teacher yet?" Joe asked jokingly.

Nick smiled. "I took your advice and I'm back, man. She's really sweet. And my dog has a major crush on her and her cat."

Joe laughed. "Good sign. Flo has pretty good judgment."

"Did you give her your medical rap sheet yet?" Joe asked.

"I gave her the CliffsNotes version."

"What'd she say?"

"Asked me if I planned to stay dead."

Joe looked at Nick thoughtfully.

"That girl's a keeper, Nick. You probably wanna try not to screw this up, man."

***

Nick spent more and more time with Sarah. One morning when they were heading toward Nick's car in the driveway, about to go to the grocery store, she saw her neighbors, Sean Gallagher and his partner, Kyle Brewer in their front yard with their golden retrievers. She waved hello and took the opportunity to introduce them to Nick.

She was explaining what they did for a living, writing, and illustrating a popular series of graphic novels, when Kyle suddenly commented, "You've got a great voice, Nick, have you ever done any acting?"

Nick laughed. "In high school. Nothing since then."

"We've been thinking about adding audio to our novels," Kyle said. "If the bug ever hits you and you'd like to do some narration, there's some pretty good money in it."

"What's 'good money' translate into these days?" Nick joked.

"About five hundred bucks an hour for a finished recording," Sean said.

"No shit?"

"And we could give you a living ton of referrals," Kyle told him. "You've got the perfect voice for this."

"I'll keep that in mind," Nick said. "Thank you."

"God, you two look great together this morning," Sean said. "And the lighting is perfect. Why don't you let me snap a photo? I'll e-mail a copy to you."

"Can I snuggle her while you're doing that?" Nick asked playfully.

"By all means," Sean replied. "Snuggle away."

And the look on their faces, the sincere affection and the playful laughter, Sean told them, made it one of the best photos he'd ever taken. He e-mailed a copy to each of them.

***

Sarah took Frank Marston's advice. She didn't call Nick. If he wanted to talk to her, he could call her. If he wanted to stay over, he could. He knew he was welcome. He was gradually learning to trust again, but it was his own decision, and at his own pace.

One morning they were sitting on the deck having coffee, when he suddenly blurted,

"I probably need to tell you some stuff."

"OK," she invited.

"You already know I'm on meds. I have to take a bunch of pills every day."

"How many?" she asked.

"About thirty."

"Yep. That's a bunch," she agreed.

"Also, I was locked up a couple of times."

"For what, drugs?" she asked.

"Hell, no. I was locked up in the psych unit because I was pretty much intent on self-harm." Nick didn't blink an eye, and his tone was casual as he spoke.

She just let him talk.

He told her about some of his nightmares.

Not all of them. But some.

"There were six of us. We were friends. We were in an up-armored Humvee equipped with CROWS, a remotely operated weapons station. That's where the gunner sits inside instead of being a friggin' target on the roof. You feel safe, you know? So, we were driving. Somebody made a joke, and we were all laughing. Paulie had the wheel. We thought the road had been swept. It hadn't been. It was mined and he hit an IED.

"I was reliving all of it, again, and again, and again," he told her. "Every single time I closed my eyes I could see the inside of the Humvee, all the blood and the body parts. Pieces of men I knew and liked. I could hear the screams. Paulie… Paulie's head landed in my lap. His eyes were open. He was looking at me."

Jeezus God Almighty, Sarah thought, but somehow, she managed to maintain her composure and continued listening without comment.

"And we accidentally killed a lot of civilians while we were there. It happened a lot, you know. We weren't supposed to talk about it. The higher ups told us not to report it. But I can still see their faces in my dreams. Some of them... were just... little kids. I've gone over and over it a million times trying to figure out if there was any way I could've known, any way I could've prevented it. One little girl... she just came out of nowhere. I registered the frightened look on her face for a fraction of a second, but I'd already pulled the trigger."

There was a haunted expression in his eyes.

"I didn't know how... to stop the dreams."

"If that was what my life was going to be like, I figured I didn't want to live. I'd rather have died with my men."

"Eventually they got me into PTSD therapy.

"It helped some. It's still helping.

"Anyway, I thought you deserved to know that."

Sarah was silent as she considered how difficult confessing to that had just been for him.

"Did you think that would make a difference in my feelings for you?" she asked softly.

"I thought maybe it might."

"Guess you don't know me very well yet," she replied.

"I'm going for a refill on my coffee," she continued casually. "Can I top yours off?"

Wordlessly he handed her his cup.

When she returned, he looked her in the eye and said, "Thank you, Sarah."

She knew what he meant.

***

"What are we watching tonight?" Nick asked. They were propped up in bed and each had a small bowl of popcorn and a coke sitting on their respective nightstands.

"My turn to pick? OK, I'll give you a choice between two: *Crazy Rich Asians* or *Unleashed*. There's a very brief scene with fireworks in *Crazy Rich Asians*. If you think that one might bother you, we can either mute the sound, or simply watch the other movie."

"Are these icky romantic chick-flicks?" he asked, with a feigned wince.

"Nope, they're light and entertaining. I think you'll like both. But if you don't, we can just watch something else. We've got a lot of choices."

While she was waiting for him to make up his mind, she picked up her hairbrush and began brushing her shoulder-length hair.

It seemed to mesmerize him.

"Can I do that?" Nick asked.

"What… pick the movie? Of course."

"No, can I brush your hair while we watch the movie?" he asked.

She handed him the hairbrush and shrugged. "Sure."

Within seconds Sarah was approaching nirvana. "Gawd that feels good. I love it when you stroke my hair and play with my hair. You literally have me purring over here."

"Scoot closer," he whispered suggestively, nuzzling her neck. "I can stroke something else that'll make you purr even louder."

***

Nick and Flo had returned to Durham to keep his appointments and Sarah was sitting at her laptop in the den working on the textbook. Maxine kept trying to drape herself over Sarah's outstretched arms.

"Maxine, baby kitty, I love you dearly, but I honest to God can't type with you lying on top of my arms like that."

Maxine just yawned. *Your point?* Seemed to be her attitude.

Exasperated with trying to dissuade the chubby cat from using her touch-typing position as a nap shelf, she shoved her chair back and Maxine promptly appropriated Sarah's lap instead.

"OK, I give up. I've been trying to avoid it but it's probably time to check in with my folks," Sarah sighed. She tried to make sure she called once a month. Subjecting herself to more than that would have been like self-flagellation.

Sarah dialed the home number and was surprised when her father answered instead of Pauline.

"Hi Dad, it's Sarah. What are you doing home? Are you feeling, OK?"

"The office is being painted. And goddamned Pauline is being a pain in the ass as usual. I should have divorced that poisonous bitch years ago. I could have had a happy life if it hadn't been for you."

"Wha?" a stunned Sarah struggled to figure out what he was talking about.

"Pauline told me you had to join a gym because you let yourself get fat," he commented. "You'll never find a husband if you get fat, Sarah. Nobody will want you."

Sarah shook her head to make sure she was hearing that properly.

"Uhhh... Dad, (A) I'm dating a very handsome Marine, and (B) I'm not fat. Jackie wears a size ten. I wear a size six. I have *always* worn a size six. The only reason I joined a gym was to get some more exercise. I spend a lot of my time indoors."

"You should have paid more attention in school," he scolded. "You should have tried to make something out of yourself. You could have made good money if only you'd applied yourself. Your sister's a nurse. She makes good money. You should try to be more like your sister," he continued. "Pauline told me you're working with children in daycare."

"I'm doing *what*?" Sarah burst out laughing. "Uhhh… Dad, I don't know where you've been, but I'm a full professor at a major university. I also earn more money than Jackie does."

"If you were really a professor, you'd be at work right now," he said dismissively.

Jeezus. "Dad… I took a year sabbatical to create a new course for the university and to write a textbook. I took a five-minute break from writing that textbook to call home and check in. Would you like me to read you the textbook page I just wrote? It's on my laptop screen. The course I'm creating is entitled Technology, Marketing, and Game Theory in the Arts. It covers the interaction between technology and the arts, the way in which words and images influence people, and the way their decisions are made. You can also pull up the university's webpage if you'd like, where you'll find not only my name and my position, but my salary. It's public record."

"Nobody will want you if you continue to let yourself get fat, Sarah."

"Uhhh… Dad, have you been drinking?"

"If it wasn't for you, I could have had a happy life. I have to go now."

Click.

What in the ever-lovin fuck was that about? Sarah wondered.

***

The nightmares. God, the nightmares. They continued to come. Not as frequently, but still just as bad.

Nick went to sleep in his bed in Durham but minutes later he was in Afghanistan, where Paulie's disembodied head was looking at him. Nick's scream startled a sleeping Flo, and he awakened soaked in ice cold sweat. Flo was instantly awake and at his side.

"Fuck!" he gasped. "*Fuck!*" He rolled out of bed and began pacing the floor, trying to get his heart rate back under control. Flo was at his side, ready for his anxiety attack.

He staggered into the bathroom, splashed cold water on his face, wet a washcloth, ran it over his sweating torso then toweled off.

As he headed back toward the bed his knees gave out. "Flo, *brace, brace!*" he yelped and tried to catch himself on the door frame. Flo broke his fall and Nick landed on the side of the bed. Gasping, he rolled over on his back and lay there staring at the ceiling.

I can't do this to Sarah, he thought to himself. *She doesn't deserve it. I'm so fucked up. I can't subject anyone else to this. It just wouldn't be fair.*

***

Nick, Joe and their buddy, another Marine, Mark Kepler, had decided to grab a quick lunch together before their PTSD meeting.

"We haven't seen much of you, man. You been, OK?" Mark asked.

"What's going on, Nick? You look a little ragged around the edges," Joe noted before turning and yelling the lunch order to their regular waitress. "Three buds on tap and burgers with fries when you get a minute, Carol."

"What's the magic word, Joe?" she called back to tease him.

"*Tip,*" he shouted back.

"That'll work," she laughed.

"Busy with a new chick?" Mark asked.

"Busy with school and Wounded Warrior and PTSD stuff, and I'm not sleeping worth a damn when I'm home."

"But you're sleeping OK when with you're with Sarah?" Joe asked perceptively.

"Yeah, but it's not fair to lead her on," Nick replied.

"Wait a minute. What does she say when she sees you with the nightmares?" Joe asked.

"Well, I haven't actually had nightmares when I'm with her."

"But you think she won't be able to handle them, right?" Mark asked.

"No. That's not the case. Nothing fazes her. She pretty much just takes me as I am, and sort of rolls with it."

Joe and Mark exchanged glances and rolled their eyes.

"Hold the phone," said Joe. "Are you seriously gonna let this girl get away from you?"

"That's the problem. I'd marry her in a minute, but she's too good for me. It's just not fair to her. I gotta stop seeing her."

"Yo, Captain Obvious," Mark said to Joe. "You wanna try explaining this to him using... oh, I don't know, puppets and crayons or something?"

"Fuck him," Joe replied. "I'm gonna ask her out myself," he joked.

Once their PTSD meeting was over Mark asked if either of them wanted to come over to play *Call of Duty*.

PTSD treatment approaches often use virtual reality technologies, which have many similarities with FPS (First Person Shooter) games like *Call of Duty*.

Both begged off, though. Joe had another appointment and Nick pleaded exhaustion. "I'm pretty beat down today, man," he told Mark. "I'll have to take a rain check."

Although Nick had Sarah's class three nights a week, he'd been showing up and giving a friendly wave, but otherwise avoiding her. Flo was not particularly amused with not being allowed to approach Sarah, and she whined softly to make her feelings known.

After the third straight class like that Sarah reached out to her friend Frank again.

"Hey Frank, Whatcha up to sweetie?"

"Sitting here cleaning my gun collection. What's going on kiddo?"

"I don't know what to do Frank. Nick is hard to read, and I honestly don't know what I should try next. Pull away? Talk about it? He's bent, we know that, PTSD, service dog, meds, and hellish nightmares. This is where you come in buddy. What do I do?"

"Pull back Sarah. If he's not ready, you can't make him. You remember we talked about this, right?"

"Yeah, I know, Frank. I was hoping for another answer."

"It is what it is. Whoops. My eBay bid is up. Gotta go kiddo. You'll be OK."

"I miss you, Buddy. Thanks."

"I miss you too sweetheart."

"Bye, Frank."

"I sure can pick 'em, can't I Maxine?" Sarah said with a sigh.

The following week Nick wasn't quite as distant.

"OK, remember people..." she addressed the class. "Your essay is due next class, e-mail me if you have any questions. Have a good weekend everybody."

Nick waited until the rest of the class had left, then headed for Sarah's desk.

"I've been knee-deep, Sarah."

"You don't owe me any explanations, Nick, you know that. Need me to sign your paper?"

He handed it to Sarah.

"Dinner tonight?" he asked.

"Sure, why not?"

"What do you feel like having... Barbeque? Italian? Chinese? Applebee's?"

"I've had a long day myself," she told him. "Why don't we just get takeout and go home and watch a movie?"

"Works for me."

"I have a yen for fish and chips," she decided.

"Applebee's it is," he said. "I'll meet you at home. Drive carefully."

After dinner they cuddled on the sofa and held hands while watching TV. Nick's legs were draped over Sarah, and when she idly stroked one of them, he physically winced.

"Forgot to tell you about that," he said. "My nerves are damaged from being blown up, and I also can't handle any pressure on my knees. They're both bad. That's one reason I have Flo and I don't use a cane. Forcing myself to use my legs instead of depending upon a cane helps keep them working. If I should suffer a seizure or trip, Flo's job is to break my fall to help me avoid head trauma."

Sarah raised Nick's hand to her lips and kissed it.

"It's gonna be OK," she reassured him.

"Lie back on my chest. I don't have a hairbrush handy, so I'm just going to play with your hair."

"Oh yeah," she purred.

Chapter Eleven

Back Home (For Today)

Sarah picked up the phone and dialed.
"Hey Girl," Ed answered.
"Hey, Ed. I could use a hug."
"Me too. Come on over. We'll grill a couple of steaks."

***

"... So that's pretty much the story, Ed," she told him.
"I've been following Frank's suggestion, letting him decide whether he's ready to rejoin the world, whether or not he's ready for a serious relationship. Unfortunately, in the meantime I really fell hard for this guy. I feel like... I don't know, I feel like I know the guy he was before he got blown up. The guy I think he still is. That probably sounds naïve. Stupid even." Sarah sighed heavily.
"Jeezus Christ." Ed shook his head. "That boy's been carryin' a bitch of a load, Sarah. Been there. Glad he's got a service dog and that he's still in treatment. Smart decision. Show's his head's still working."

Sarah had made herself comfortable in one of the chairs out at the fire pit, as Ed placed a pair of steaks on the grill.

"What's your guy's last name?" Ed asked.

"Bowman. Nick Bowman. Why?"

Ed sighed. "Shit. Once you started telling me about his background, I thought maybe that's who it was."

"You know him?" Sarah asked curiously.

"This part of the world's not all that big, I've lived here a long time and I know a whole lot of people," Ed commented.

"I've known Nick Bowman's family for years. They're real good people, Sarah. And I remember Nick when he was growing up. Smart as a whip, good natured kid. I ran into his dad a few months ago. We both happened to be in Raleigh on business.

"His father said the Marines hadn't been all that forthcoming with the families of wounded warriors, and he'd been pretty ticked off about it. They told him that Nick had been wounded in Afghanistan, and that was pretty much it.

"Nick called 'em once or twice, downplayed the situation, told them he was OK and he was being shuffled from hospital to hospital, country to country, and state to state for a while and that it was just routine. Nick assured his father he was coming along just fine, told them that he hadn't lost any limbs or digits, said his face hadn't been disfigured, and that he'd still be able to sire children.

"I seriously doubt his folks have any idea his wounds, as extensive as you've just told me they are, were more than physical. Brett Bowman, that's his father, told me Nick calls home occasionally now, but as far as I know Brett hasn't actually seen his son since he shipped out several years ago.

"Nick told me he hadn't gone to see his family since he'd been back because he didn't want to have to see the pity in their eyes," Sarah volunteered.

"Aw, Jeez," Ed lamented, shaking his head.

"Girl, I'm gonna tell you the same thing Frank did. Ain't nobody gonna be able to bring this boy back from the edge if he's not ready to take that step himself.

"My advice is don't put any pressure on him, God knows the boy's got enough on his plate already. And you want to be real careful not to set him back, Sarah. You just go right ahead and live your life. If and when he's ready, he'll come to you."

"Got it," she nodded.

"You still in touch with your family?" he asked, changing the subject.

"I call home maybe once a month. Why do I still do that? I have no idea. I certainly don't need the aggravation, but for some reason I do it anyway. I suppose I keep hoping for acceptance. It doesn't happen. The conversation with my mother doesn't usually last more than two maybe three minutes tops. Just long enough for her to either ignore or insult me. I gotta stop doing that. It's not good for my head.

"But you know, the last time I called home, a couple of weeks ago I think it was, my father answered the phone, and it was a really, really weird conversation."

"So, tell me."

"He said he was home during the day because his office was being painted and then he just blurted out, 'Pauline is being a pain in the ass as usual. I should have divorced that poisonous bitch years ago' and 'I could have had a happy life if it hadn't been for you.'"

"So that was pretty weird, but then he said, 'Pauline told me you had to join a gym because you let yourself get fat,' so by this point my jaw had dropped and then he said she'd told him that I was 'working with students in daycare.'"

Sarah started laughing as she related the bizarre conversation.

"So, then he started in on me, scolding me for not having paid enough attention in school," Sarah giggled again. "Oh yeah, and he said I should have tried to be more like my sister so I could have been earning decent money. I swear it was like being in the twilight zone."

"How did you respond?" Ed asked curiously.

"I think I asked if he'd been drinking."

Ed laughed out loud.

"I told him Jackie wore a size ten and I'd always worn a size six, and I told him I was a full professor at a major university and that my salary was larger than hers. He didn't believe me. So, I suggested he look me up on the university's website, and I told him he could also verify my salary on that website, because it was matter of public record."

"What did he say to that?"

"He said he had to go, and hung up on me." She burst out laughing again.

"It was just really, really weird, Ed."

"Yes," Ed agreed, his eyes narrowing thoughtfully. "Yes, it was."

***

Ed slowly pulled the Caddy into the dirt and gravel parking lot, parked, beeped the doors locked, walked in the building and glanced around. The juke box was playing, but at a softer volume than it usually was during evening hours when the place was packed.

"*Ed!*" came a shout from across the room. "You old son-of-a-bitch, Come on back here!"

Ed burst out laughing, Big Lou stood and when Ed reached the table the two men shared a bear hug with back slaps. "How the hell you been, buddy? Pull up a chair, my friend, how about a cold beer?"

Ed grinned. "Whatcha got on tap, darlin'?" he hollered to Karen, the affable busty bleached blonde behind the bar. "You got Narragansett?"

"Comin' right up, sugar," she hollered back.

"So, what can I do ya for, old friend?" Lou asked.

"I noticed a few months back that you stopped by my place for a few minutes when Sarah Watson was still renting my 5th Wheel. The door was left open and it was a fairly short visit so I figured you weren't dating."

"She's a good kid, Ed. I just kinda adopted her. Tried to make sure she stayed safe. What about you?"

"Pretty much the same thing. I took on the job of helping her get her head together, getting her act back on track. She rarely drinks at all now, she quit dating losers, paid off her car and cards, and rented a house in Cary with an option to buy. She adopted a friendly old black Labrador she became real fond of, but he got cancer and had to be put down. Damn near broke her heart. Girl cried for days.

"She came back home to my place and stayed in the guest room for a couple of weeks to get over it. When she went back home, one of her neighbors gave her a big old fat cat named Maxine, that she's busy spoiling rotten, and she's dating Brett Bowman's son, Nick, a Marine. I think you know the family.

"The boy got hurt pretty bad in Afghanistan. Not sure whether it's gonna work out between them. Nick's still struggling with PTSD. He was the only survivor of a six-man crew when their Humvee hit an IED. It was... pretty messy.

"I'm told he hasn't seen his parents since he shipped out several years ago, so Brett's apparently unaware of what the boy's been struggling with. Nick calls and downplays things. You know the drill, you're standing on the ledge of the eighty-eighth floor, thinking of jumping but still telling everybody things are fine."

Big Lou nodded. "Yep. A lot of us have been there."

"Tell me about it," Ed sighed.

"At the moment Sarah's officially on a one-year sabbatical, she's creating a new course for the university and writing the textbook. But she's also teaching a night course three nights a week. He's in her class."

"Anyway, I don't know whether you're familiar with her background, her family, and that's actually what I wanted to talk to you about…"

Ed lowered his voice. "You still connected?"

"Yeah," Lou replied, equally quietly.

"Then I'm gonna tell you what I know, and what I suspect."

***

Three weeks passed without hearing from Nick. He'd show up in class, do his work, then leave. There wasn't even as much as a friendly wave. She took a deep breath and assumed the logical. *Guess it's over,* she thought, and the flame went out, not with a bang, but with a whimper.

It was a Wednesday, and this was the final class of the semester. Nick and Flo arrived and as usual he took a seat toward the back of the classroom. After a curious glance she carefully averted her eyes, looking down at her grade book when he gave no indication of wanting to make a connection. Other students were still arriving.

"Hey, Teach, you look a little tired today," remarked the skinny kid in a T-shirt and jeans.

"Yes indeed. Thanks for sharing, Travis," Sarah commented drolly. The kid chuckled.

A second student, this one built like a football player, made a similar observation.

"Hi Professor. Rough night?"

"Thank you for noticing, GenDarius," she replied sarcastically.

Sarah handed stacks of the exam to three people and asked them to start passing them out.

"Everybody got a copy?" she asked a few minutes later, looking around the room to make certain.

"OK, then, let's get started. Put your notes away and take out a pen. You can leave after you're finished with the exam. Good luck, group."

Nick was one of the first to walk up to her desk and turn in his exam. He reached out to hand Sarah the exam but instead of taking it she nodded toward the box where the finished exams were to be placed. He next handed her the attendance sheet for her signature.

She quickly scribbled her name and the date and handed it back to him. A second student attempted to hand her his paper. Again, she nodded toward the exam box.

"Have a great day," Nick ventured, before turning and heading out.

Sarah didn't reply. She continued to grade papers.

When she finally did look up Nick had already left the room.

She gathered the finished exams and straightened the stack, accepting the last two submissions from a pair of stragglers.

She forced a smile. "Have a great day," she told them.

It was around seven that evening when Sarah heard a light knock on the front door. She carefully lifted Maxine off her lap and deposited her on the sofa where the two of them had been watching a movie.

She glanced through the peephole, saw Nick standing there and opened the door.

"Hi," he said awkwardly.

"Hi yourself, stranger," she replied.

"Can I come in?"

"Of course."

Flo shoved her way forward.

"Hello, you precious baby girl," Sarah said, leaning over and affectionately snuffling Flo, giving her a head-boop while scratching behind both of her ears. Flo's tail beat wildly.

"What's up, Nick. Come on in and sit down. What was it that you wanted?" she asked curiously.

"I'm not really sure."

"OK," she said agreeably.

Sarah sat silently, waiting for Nick to say whatever it was he had planned to say.

"I know it's been a few days, but I've been busy with wounded warrior and other shit. I've just been beat down is all."

"So, you're not sleeping?" she asked.

"No. Too much on my mind, I guess."

"Anything I can help with?" she offered.

"I think… I need to stop seeing you."

"OK" she said.

He looked startled.

"That's all you have to say is, OK?"

"You're a grown-up, Nick. This is your decision."

He sighed and looked at her sadly.

"I have to do this," he explained.

She rose from the couch. "Take care of yourself, Nick."

He didn't seem to know what else to do, so he stood and headed for the door. Flo looked back and forth at the both of them, then went to Sarah's side and lay decisively down on the floor.

"You appear to have a mutiny on your hands," Sarah observed wryly.

Maxine hopped down from the couch and lay between Flo's front paws, the two of them presenting a united front.

Nick rolled his eyes. "Fuck," he muttered. "*Flo!*"

The dog immediately jumped to her feet, sending Maxine tumbling and prompting her to deliver an annoyed hiss at Nick.

"And *now* you've pissed off Flo's cat," Sarah observed dryly.

Nick laughed, despite himself. He took a deep breath.

"Bye, Sarah," he said softly and quietly pulled the door shut behind him as he left.

She didn't cry. She'd actually been expecting this. Both Frank and Ed had told her it might happen. But it didn't really feel real yet. She guessed it might take a while. She still felt him, whatever the hell that means, she thought.

But her heart was so heavy in her chest that it literally felt like lead.

***

A half-hour later her phone rang. Pauline was on the line and she was holding back tears.

"What's the matter, Mom?"

"You need to come home. Your grandmother died this morning."

"Oh my God. Are you OK?"

Pauline dissolved into great wracking sobs. "No. I need you here," she insisted.

"Mom, I haven't seen anyone in eight years."

"The funeral is Saturday at noon. You better be here. I can't talk any more. When I die one day, you'll understand."

"All right. I'll see you in a few days."

Sarah disconnected and started checking flight availability. She settled on a flight that would get her there late Friday afternoon, then reserved a car and a hotel room. She might be willing to play dutiful daughter, but there was no way in hell she was going to volunteer to spend the night in that house.

Sarah's next call was to Ed to let him know she'd be out of town for a couple of days.

"Got somebody to take care of the cat?" he asked. "I'll take her if you don't," he volunteered.

"You're a sweetheart, Ed. I'm going to ask my neighbors across the street if they'll do it. They're the ones who gave her to me. All of her food and litter stuff is already here, and I'll leave the TV on, so she won't feel lonely. If they're not available, I'll take you up on your offer."

"You ready to put yourself on the firing line?" Ed asked. "Because I fear that's exactly what you're doing."

"Yeah, I know. But what kind of a human being would I be to refuse that kind of request?" she asked him.

"OK but just remember I'm only a phone call away and I'm here for you."

"I love you to death, Ed."

"Ditto, girl."

***

When Ed got off the phone with Sarah, he dialed another number.

"We got anything yet?" he inquired, and then explained why he was asking.

"I'll take care of it," Big Lou replied.

Chapter Twelve

The Truth (Always Comes Out)

About an hour later, Sarah and Maxine sat on the couch, watching the rest of the movie they'd been watching earlier, and nursing a glass of wine she was not particularly interested in finishing when the phone rang. The caller ID that appeared was Big Lou.

She smiled and answered, "Hey there, stranger!"

"Hey yourself. How've you been? Haven't seen much of you lately."

"I've been trying to get my act together."

"Atta girl! You gonna be around for a couple of minutes? I've got something for you and I'm right around the corner. May I swing by? I can't stay long, I've gotta get back to the bar. Got some business I need to attend to."

"Sure, come on ahead. But I'm not in the stupid 5th wheel any more," she laughed. "I'm about ten minutes from there. I've got a little house in Cary. Let me give you the address. I'll turn the outside light on."

A few minutes later, Sarah heard the low rumble of Lou's bike followed by a knock at the door. She opened the door with a delighted smile and threw her arms around Lou's neck.

"How the hell are you, darlin'? Whatcha got there?" she asked, nodding at a manila folder in Lou's hands. "Come sit down, what's your pleasure, beer? Wine? A shot?"

"I don't need a thing; pretty girl and you know I don't drink and drive."

"Good man!" she said with a smile.

"Have a seat," she offered.

Lou looked around. "Come on over here," he suggested, nodding toward the sofa.

"You sound serious," she said.

"Maybe," he shrugged, as the two of them sat down at opposite ends of the sofa, then angled themselves toward the center, the manila folder lay on a cushion between them.

"What?" Sarah began.

"You remember a while back when you told me that if I ever figured out why your family treated you like shit, you'd want me to tell you?"

Sarah looked at him, stunned into silence by his comment. She nodded slowly.

"This is your choice, Sarah. If you truly want to know, I have the answers for you. You don't have to do this if you don't want to. We can walk over to your fireplace and set this folder on fire, and we'll never speak of it again. As far as I'm concerned, this conversation will never have happened. Again, this is nobody's choice but yours."

Sarah looked at him, the blood draining from her face. "Whooo," she exhaled. "Now here's something I hadn't expected. On the other hand, your timing is right on the money. I'm supposed to fly up there on Friday and I'm definitely not looking forward to it. So yeah, whatever you've got, I think it's time that I heard it."

"Go for it," she sighed, and made herself comfortable.

"Your mother's name was Suzie Smith. She was a widow. Her husband had been killed toward the end of the Iran-Iraq War. That was the First Gulf War. She was a very pretty, very bright young woman. She was the office manager for a fairly good-sized business. She fell in love with her boss. It was the usual thing, she was lonely, he told her he planned to leave his wife, and he had indeed planned to do exactly that. She got pregnant and although the timing was a bit awkward, she wanted to keep the baby. He hadn't yet gotten around to telling his wife he wanted a divorce.

"Suzie quit her job before she began to show, or people would have talked. She tactfully gave the excuse that she had to go take care of an elderly relative. Her boss owned some nice townhouses in the next county that his wife didn't know about, so he set Suzie up in one of those and continued paying her salary. She was still doing work for the company, so that made the continued expense easier to explain.

"The wife thought that he was out of town for a few days on business, but he was actually with Suzie. She went into labor early, and he rushed her to the hospital, the one in the next county, where it was unlikely, he'd run into any of his clients.

"As it turned out, Suzie had been hemorrhaging internally for the better part of a day and a half without being aware of it. She had been on total bed rest with near complete lack of movement. She wasn't due to deliver for another two weeks. Hemorrhagic placenta previa is typically characterized by painless third trimester bleeding.

"Emergency room physicians examined her using ultrasound upon arrival and recognized the gravity of the situation. They immediately had both Suzie and her boss, your biological father, sign an acknowledgment of paternity affidavit, a legal form parents complete to add the biological father's name to the child's birth certificate. By signing the form, parents are establishing paternity for their child — meaning legally recognized fatherhood. That form protects the child in the event something goes wrong.

"They then rushed Suzie into surgery, did an emergency C-section and were just barely able to save your life. Although the surgeons gave it everything they had, they were not able to save Suzie. You were placed in the neonatal ward and carefully monitored for three weeks.

"Suzie was an only child. Her parents died in an automobile crash several years earlier. Your only living relative was Suzie's boss, your biological father. Who was still married.

"He faced a number of emotions. He was grief stricken by Suzie's death, terrified that his wife would find out he had been having an affair, resentful that he had been saddled with a pretty major problem, worried that the situation, if the news got out, might have a negative effect on his business.

"Putting the child up for adoption seemed like the logical solution."

Sarah had been listening carefully. She nodded at Lou, indicating that she clearly understood what had transpired.

"What did she look like?" Sarah asked quietly. "Does anyone still have a picture of her?"

Big Lou nodded, pulled a color snapshot from the manila folder and handed it to her.

"My God, we could have been twins!" Sarah gasped.

Lou smiled. "Both very beautiful women."

"Could... could I keep this?" Sarah asked him.

"Of course," he nodded.

"Shall I continue?" he asked.

Sarah looked startled. "There's more?"

"Uh-huh," Lou confirmed.

"Your biological father owned a successful business, and he was accustomed to looking at situations logically, examining multiple alternatives to any problem. He had realized by this point that by willingly signing the acknowledgment of paternity affidavit, he had blown any chance of denying the fact that he was the father.

"He was married and if he were to get a divorce, he might be risking one hell of a lot of money. Especially under these circumstances. Thank God he and his wife had no children together, he thought. He could have been on the hook for child support, as well as alimony. Still, depending upon the judge, he might lose his home. He might even lose his business. Not good.

"Had Suzie lived, he realized, it might have been a different story. He really had loved Suzie. The two of them working together could easily have rebuilt his career had he divorced his wife and gotten financially hammered in a divorce.

"There was also the problem of the child. With continuing DNA advancements, the grown child might one day simply show up at the door wanting to meet her father. That could be an ugly scene since he's married. If he wanted to leave her something, he'd have to put her in his will and then even more questions would be asked. Another potentially ugly scene.

"If he chose to arrange for the child to be adopted the adopting parents would be told who the biological parents were. He didn't like that idea very much either.

"So, he decided to make a semi-clean breast of the situation, admit to his wife that he had strayed but not admit that it had been a long-term thing or that he had loved Suzie. He'd just say it was a one-night stand and that the woman had refused to get an abortion. He'd ask his wife for advice on how best to handle the baby problem. He'd beg her forgiveness, offer to make amends by buying her a new house and putting it in her name. She always responded well to financial inducements and the idea of a luxury home in her name only ought to do the trick, he thought. He had other investments she knew nothing about and there was nothing that said he had to put a large down payment on the new place.

"So that's how he presented it to her. An apology, an offer of a luxury home in her own name, and she could decide how to get shed of the baby problem."

"So, the wife told her husband that under the circumstances, she thought adoption would be the best course of action."

Big Lou paused to make certain Sarah was following.

Again, Sarah nodded.

"But she completely blindsided her husband by saying that she and her husband should be the ones to take the baby."

Sarah blinked and her mouth dropped open.

"Holy *fuck!*" she shouted at the top of her lungs.

"Holy muther-fucking *bastards!*" she yelled. "That miserable goddamned bitch kept me to torture both me *and* my father and in the process, she taught him to *hate* me!"

"And together… together, those psychos taught my half-sister Jackie to hate me as well!"

"Jeezus H. Christ! What kind of sick fucks *are* these people!"

"Oh my God. Oh my God. I don't have to do this any more." she gasped, then gulped, then broke into deep sobs. "I don't have to do this any more," she wept, as Lou reached into a pocket, pulled out a pair of crisply ironed white linen handkerchiefs, handed them to her, then gathered her in his arms and let her cry it out.

It took a while.

"I never have to go back there," she sobbed in relief. "Never. I never have to see those horrible people ever again. Fuck them! Fuck them all!" she sobbed again.

Then she started to laugh. "Since when do you carry expensive linen handkerchiefs?" She wiped her eyes and blew her nose then asked with a giggle.

"I can handle myself in polite company, and I've been known to get dressed up on occasion," he replied with a twinkle in his eye.

"But how?"

"I still have some connections," he replied cryptically. "You already know one of them."

"You're not going to expand on that answer, are you?" Sarah giggled through a tearful hiccup and hugged him again.

"Nope," he said flatly, but with a hint of a smile.

"Thank you, Lou. Thank you from the bottom of my heart."

"What are you going to do now, Sarah," he asked.

Sarah took a deep cleansing breath, still punctuated by the gasps and involuntary flutters that often follow heavy weeping.

"I am going to move forward with my life, Lou," she announced firmly.

"I am going to move forward."

"Are you still going to go to the funeral this weekend?" he asked.

Startled, she looked at him.

"I didn't tell you about the funeral," she said suspiciously. "You know Ed."

He winced. "Known him for years. He's a close friend."

"I love you both."

"And we love you."

"So, you didn't answer the question. What are you going to do about the funeral?" he asked again.

"I don't know," she mused. "I'm gonna have to think about it. Whatever I decide, thanks to the two of you, I think I'm prepared to deal with just about anything."

***

Surprisingly, Sarah actually slept fairly well that night. Before she went to bed however, she scanned her mother's photo and emailed it to her phone. *I'm sorry I never had the chance to know you Mommy,* she thought.

And now I understand what Dad meant. Had it not been for the accidental pregnancy he could have divorced Pauline, married my mother Suzie, they'd have been happy and could have waited until the time was right to have a child together.

Dad was also right about Pauline. She is a poisonous bitch. So is Jackie for that matter. I seriously doubt that I'll ever be able to have a relationship with my father, but at least now I understand why.

And I also know exactly what I want to do next, she decided.

I wonder if I can find what I need?

***

Sarah drove the FedEx envelope directly to the ship center early Thursday morning. She wanted to make certain it would be delivered to her father and nobody else. Toward that end she had addressed the waybill to Matthew Watson at his office address. A recipient only signature was required, which meant that it had to be personally signed for by the addressee, and not a secretary, and an ID would have to be shown to the driver. Sarah had also insured the contents of the envelope for a thousand dollars, simply as a precaution to ensure extra careful handling. It was sent FedEx First Overnight® for Friday morning delivery.

Inside were two eight x ten inch photographs.

In order to create what she'd wanted to send; she had searched for an early public relations shot of her father. He'd been a very handsome man back then. And he looked happy. No wonder her mother had fallen in love with him, she thought.

Sarah had also been able to find an old kindergarten photo of herself. The photographer must have said something funny because she'd been laughing happily in the shot.

She had asked Sean Gallagher, across the street, to refer her to a Photoshop expert and explained what she wanted to do. Sean was an expert himself and offered to create exactly what she was looking for. She watched, fascinated, as he manipulated those two images plus the photograph of her pretty, smiling mother, turning them into what looked for all the world like a studio photograph of a happy family. Her father, her mother, and herself as a child. He'd printed it on photograph stock for her and he'd made two copies. One for her to keep, one to give as a gift. He also sent a digital image to her.

The second photo in the FedEx envelope was an enlargement of the same photo he'd personally taken of a slim and petite Sarah next to a tall and handsome Nick with her new house in the background, the flowers all in bloom, the lighting perfect, and the look of love in their eyes.

Along with those two photos, Sarah had enclosed a simple note to her father.

'I will not be attending the funeral for Pauline's mother.

I finally understand, Dad.

And yes, you were almost right.

The three of us really could have been happy.

Sarah.'

Sarah handed the envelope to the counter agent, took a deep breath, and went on with her life.

Chapter Thirteen

Wide Open (Military Style)

One evening, a few weeks later, Sarah stopped by a local restaurant intending to order takeout. She was standing in the otherwise empty lobby gazing upward at the list of offerings accompanied by slick photos of appealing dinners, when an attractive man tentatively approached her.

"Professor Watson?"

She turned and saw a face that looked vaguely familiar and struggled for a moment to put a name to the face.

"Joe Anderson, isn't it?" she asked him with a smile. "And I think that at this point you can probably just call me Sarah."

"How've you been, Joe? What have you been up to?" she asked cheerfully.

Instead of answering right away, he said, "Have you got plans? If not, why don't we grab one of the tables on the patio and let me buy you dinner."

Sarah hesitated.

"We're already here and I don't bite. Honest," Joe assured her softly.

She smiled. "Well in that case..."

The two of them headed for a table away from the noisiest part of the outdoor dining area so they wouldn't have to shout to be heard.

"Are you still teaching at the university?" he asked.

She nodded. "I'm actually close to winding up a sabbatical. I took a year off to create a new course for the university and write a textbook. I completed the book yesterday. I want to give it one more quick look to make sure I haven't missed anything, and then it will go to the textbook publisher."

"How about you?" she asked. "What have you been up to since you were in my class all those years ago?"

"Did a few tours in the military, got shot up a few times, decided I wasn't having any fun, and when they offered to give me an honorable discharge, I took them up on it.

"I own a computer related business in Raleigh, do some work for the government, got a few people working for me. I've also been doing some investing here and there. Overall, I've generally been leading a fairly boring life."

"Married? Kids?" she asked.

He shook his head. "Still single, after all these years."

"You?" he asked.

"There was someone I was very much in love with," she told him. "One day several months ago he just walked away. Never gave me an explanation. Stopped by one evening, said he'd decided he had to end it… and left. I never saw him again." She shrugged.

Jeezus. Joe thought to himself. *Nick, you total asshole.*

"So?" Joe waited for Sarah to finish.

She laughed. "So now I live with my cat and I work all the time."

"You're not dating anyone?" he asked.

She shook her head no. This last one took kind of a lot out of me, Joe. I feel… I guess the phrase is I feel… pretty beat down. It's probably going to take me a while before I'm ready to go through that kind of thing again."

"If he changed his mind, would you take him back?" Joe asked curiously.

"He's still in the number one position," she admitted.

Joe reached into his pocket for a ballpoint pen, then pulled a paper napkin from the dispenser on the table. She watched him curiously. He wrote the number two on the front of the napkin and his e-mail address on the back and slid it over to her.

"I'd like to be considered if the idiot in the number one position doesn't show up pretty soon," he said.

Sarah picked up the napkin, glanced at both sides, smiled, then tucked it in her purse.

"It might be a while, Joe."

"Doesn't matter. I'll wait."

"Evenin' folks. Sorry for the delay. May I take your order?" the cheerful waitress asked.

***

Joe Anderson was shopping. Shopping was definitely not his favorite thing, but he needed to pick up a new sports jacket, so he'd gone to the mall. Fortunately, it wasn't very crowded on weekdays, so he'd been able to get in and out fairly quickly. He carried the lightweight vinyl garment bag containing the jacket by the protruding hanger and had the bag slung over his shoulder.

As he walked down the wide aisle between rows of stores on his way to main doors which led to the parking lot, he caught sight of Nick Bowman seated on one of the benches in the median. Flo lay on the tile floor by his side.

Joe swerved and headed for the bench, grabbing a seat next to him and draping the bag over the seat back.

"Hey buddy, how ya been? Nobody's seen you in ages. What have you been up to?" Joe asked. "Hey Flo! What a good girl you are." Flo stood and wagged her entire butt in delight.

Nick smiled faintly and shook Joe's hand. "Hey, Joe!" Nick automatically glanced toward the adjacent store where a man and a woman stood about ten feet apart. The woman, an attractive brunette, was looking at a sparkling display of engagement rings. The man stood several feet away, looking at men's luxury watches.

"Oooh, honey I like this one," the brunette loudly called over her shoulder, pointing to a ridiculously glittering ring with a price tag equivalent to a compact car. "And I am *so* worth it!" she preened. "Oh wait, this other one's bigger. No… I like the bigger one better!"

Joe glanced at the woman and then at the man who was studiously ignoring the woman and still looking at watches.

"Jeezus. Poor bastard," Joe scoffed. Nodding toward the man looking at the watches, he joked softly to Nick. "Somebody should probably warn him that the bitch he's with is a gold digger. Run away, run away," Joe laughed as he parroted a line from *Monty Python and The Holy Grail*.

"Fool needs to bail while he still has a chance. Day-yum!" Joe marveled, looking at the guy and shaking his head in amazement, "You'd have to be a fucking idiot not to see *this* broad for what she is."

Joe didn't notice Nick's eyes widen slightly.

Just then a woman walked out the doors of the jewelry store, smiled as she approached the man looking at the watches, gave him a kiss on the cheek, took his arm and the two of them walked away.

"Nick! I'm *talking* to you!"

The brunette impatiently stamped her foot and called over her shoulder, "Honey! Hurry *up!*" she whined. "Come look at *this* one!"

Utterly dumfounded, Joe turned to look at Nick. There was a look of astonishment on Joe's face.

"I started having problems again. The doctor told me that in his opinion all I really needed was a good woman by my side, and I'd be fine," Nick reluctantly confessed.

"Have you lost your fucking *mind?*" an outraged Joe spoke in an undertone.

The brunette noticed that Nick was talking to someone and hurried over to join them. She seated herself next to Nick and possessively grabbed his arm. Flo growled softly.

"Honey aren't you going to introduce me?"

"Joe Anderson, this is Rachel McCowen."

"Hello Rachel," Joe said politely.

"So how do you two know each other?" Rachel asked Joe.

Joe caught a warning glance. Presumably he hadn't shared all that much of his past with this woman.

"We went to school together a million years ago," Joe replied vaguely.

"How about you, Rachel? Do you work around here?" Joe asked curiously.

"I did. But Nick doesn't want me to have to work any more, do you sweetheart?"

Nick's eyes looked a little glassy to Joe.

"We should get together for dinner some time," Rachel bubbled. "Are you married, or do you have a steady girlfriend, Joe?"

"There is someone special in my life, yes," Joe replied. "But Sarah's rushing to finish a textbook she's been writing, so her schedule is a little tight right now. We did manage to hit Ribsters for dinner recently, but for the most part we've been having dinner at home."

Joe watched a Nick's face suddenly flush red and saw flicker of jealous rage flash in his eyes.

Joe abruptly stood, picking up the garment bag with his jacket inside. "Well Rachel, I enjoyed meeting you. Nick, good to see you again. I gotta run, man." Joe waved over his shoulder as he hurried away.

As he walked away Joe thought to himself, *Well, I didn't exactly lie. We did have dinner at Ribsters and both Sarah and I have been having dinner at home since then. Not together, of course, we have dinner at our respective homes. But if this stupid bastard doesn't get a clue really fast and dump that gold digging airhead Rachel, I absolutely am going to start courting Sarah. I would marry that girl in a heartbeat. And I swear to God, Nick Bowman is a fucking idiot.*

***

Nick pleaded exhaustion and much to Rachel's annoyance declined to do any more shopping. She returned to the window display and Nick found himself looking at photos on his phone. He stopped at a picture of Sarah, then stopped again at the photo Sean had taken of the two of them. That one had always been his favorite. He heard Rachel approaching and he quickly put his phone way. He rose as she approached. "I'm tired, Rachel. I need to go home now."

When they got back to Nick's townhouse, he poured himself a glass of orange juice and sat down at the kitchen table, once again looking through the photos on his phone.

He quickly switched it off when Rachel joined him at the table.

"Seems like you're falling more and more," she commented.

"Is that a problem Rachel?" he asked somewhat tightly.

"No, of course not."

"Sure, seems like it," he said, and annoyed, he rose and walked off, with Flo shadowing him.

Nick had visited his neurosurgeon recently.

"Looks like the shrapnel has moved about a millimeter, Nick," Dr. Jacobs told him, as he looked through the imaging reports. "Given your migraine frequency and pain increase and loss of balance, that makes sense. We'll need to adjust your meds and manage the pain. Young man, on a personal note, I hope you've locked down good woman to help you weather these occasional adjustments."

"I hope so too, sir," Nick said thoughtfully.

His second appointment that day had been with his psychiatrist.

"You livin' in this hospital boy?" his nurse joked. "I've been seein' you up and down these halls all day."

"Yes ma'am. I'm just takin' care of business," he joked.

But when he was actually in the office, Nick's tone was no longer jocular.

"Doc, my migraines have increased and some days I can't move my legs. You know I wanted to die when I was lying in the hospital after being blown up. I couldn't walk, my knees were blown out, five surgeries later, constant pain. Nerve damage in my legs. I went from being a straight-A student to struggling to identify fucking reality. I can't ride my Harley, hunt, skydive, fly. Hell, I'm lucky if I remember my meds or what I had for lunch. My nightmares cause me flashbacks and cold sweats. I was honorably discharged, and I earned a shit load of medals which don't mean squat. I have nothing if I no longer have a decent life. Tell me Doc, who in their right mind would want any part of this? Is there assisted suicide in our state?"

The doctor reached out and grasped both of Nick's shoulders. "Son, let me tell you something. You're lucky. You're damned lucky. You walked through the fucking valley of death, and you beat the bastard. You have more looks and stamina than ninety-nine percent of the warriors who make it this far.

"Somewhere out there is a woman who will love you exactly as you are and knock herself out to make you happy. She's not going to be a taker, boy. She's going to be a giver. You keep a lookout for that woman, and when you find her, you grab her, because that kind of gal is as rare as hen's teeth. She won't care if you're a little bent. And aren't we all?" he laughed.

"I'll see you next month, Nick. If you need me before then, you give me a call. Seriously, I'm here for you anytime you need me."

***

Nick and Rachel were sitting in aluminum folding chairs on the back patio of Nick's townhouse. He had the grill going and it was just about time to take the steaks off the fire.

Flo sat statue-still at Nick's side, silently glaring at Rachel.

Nick stood, grabbed the tongs and was about to head for the grill. He paused and asked Rachel to hand him the plate for the steaks.

Rachel grabbed the plate from the table and held it out. Nick lost his center of balance and grabbed for the lightweight lawn chair which promptly tipped. Flo instinctively moved into position which kept Nick from falling, but the plate hit the hard concrete patio floor and shattered.

"Jesus, Nick," Rachel snapped in exasperation. "What's next? Another migraine this evening?"

Flo narrowed her eyes and growled softly at Rachel.

Rachel stamped off to the kitchen and brought back another plate, as well as a broom and dustpan.

"Just put my steak in the refrigerator please, Rachel. I'm not feeling very well. I think I need to go lie down."

"What are you, fucking eighty years old with your goddamn nap shit?" Rachel muttered under her breath, but out of earshot of Nick's hearing.

Flo sat straight up, narrowed her eyes and glared at Rachel. Nick sighed heavily, went to stand up and began to lose his balance.

"Brace, brace Flo. Brace," Nick yelped.

Rachel not bothering to move, sat frozen, staring at Flo as the dog moved quickly to break Nick's fall.

***

As Nick lay in bed resting, he pulled out his phone and flipped through pictures again. He stared for a very long time at Sarah's photo then shook his head and switched to browser mode.

He then began researching engagement rings.

He gave the whole situation a great deal of thought. Eventually he made his decision, ordering the custom-made diamond semi-mount from one diamond dealer, and the solitaire from another. He'd seen what appealed to Rachel in the jewelry store window, which appeared to be the gaudier the better. At the same time, he didn't want it to be ridiculously ostentatious.

The diamond semi-mount he ordered would be custom designed to accept a ten-millimeter diamond. Total carat weight in this ring would be 4.37 carats. The diamonds were superb VS clarity with top white E color. The style was described as a double halo designed to surround a center diamond. The round halo of diamonds was then itself surrounded by a square halo of diamonds, with additional diamonds flowing halfway down the ring shank from each side of the halo. He specified next day delivery for both. He'd hand carry both packages to the local jeweler who would carefully mount the center then photograph and appraise the sparkling diamond engagement ring for insurance purposes. The ring really was a knock-out. He thought it absurdly flashy. *But Rachel is gonna love it,* he thought.

He had the finished ring back the same day. He gave it to her the following morning. He didn't ask her to marry him, he just gave her the pretty little gift-wrapped velvet box with the big bow on it.

She shrieked with joy and threw her arms around him.

When she finally settled down, he decided that was the time to solicit her thoughts about the wedding itself.

"I'd prefer a small wedding, Rachel."

"Are you crazy?" she shouted angrily. "This is *my* day, Nick. I want a *huge* wedding."

"I'm going get something to drink," he told her. "Can I bring you something?"

"No," she said dismissively.

But when he started to rise, his knees began to give out. "Flo *brace, brace!*" he shouted, and Flo rushed to his side, accidentally shoving Rachel out of the way in her haste to get to Nick in time.

"Fucking goddamn dog," Rachel snarled under her breath.

In a lowered voice she was certain Nick could not hear, she angrily snapped, "You better not fall during *my* wedding, Nick Bowman."

A short time later, Nick received a call from his buddy Joe. He was in the neighborhood and asked if Nick wanted to grab lunch and a beer. Joe was angling for an opportunity to try to talk some sense into Nick.

"Sure Joe. Sounds good. Listen, while you're here can you glance at my laptop and tell me whether I need to take it to the shop or just throw the damn thing in the trash and buy a new one?"

Joe laughed. "Sure thing."

Joe arrived just as Rachel was about to go back to her place, but she was thrilled with the opportunity to show off her new ring.

"Look, look, *look,* Joe!" Rachel shouted excitedly, holding up her left hand when she opened the door to let him in.

"Jeezus. That's a helluva rock, Rachel," a stunned Joe commented.

Rachel whirled and waved as she headed out the door. "Gotta run Joe. Bye!"

Hearing all the commotion, Nick thumped down the stairs preceded by the ever-mindful Flo.

"Hey, Joe."

"You gave her a ring. You gave Rachel a ring," Joe said in disbelief.

"Yeah, but…"

"What the *fuck* is the matter with you, man?" Joe yelled. "What happened with Sarah, Nick?"

Stunned by the unexpected outburst, Nick stood silent, his mouth slightly open.

"You kicked her to the curb, you son of a bitch. For *what?* That piece of shit gold digger who couldn't hold a fucking *candle* to Sarah?"

"What branch of service were you in?" Joe shouted.

"Marines, asshole," Nick retorted with a frown. "And you just wait one goddamned minute, Joe."

"Fuck you, Nick. You served four tours in Iraq, got blown up and fucking survived brother."

Joe pointed his finger at Nick and yelled even louder.

"How much death have you seen? How many fucking brothers have you seen blown up who never had a chance to return home to their families? Yet you have the fucking audacity to walk away from a woman that loves you exactly the way you are, broke down and beat down. You… you… sorry-assed son of a bitch!

"You have no fucking right calling yourself a fellow Marine. All of your brothers that died, all the ones who never had a chance for their wives and kids to hug them again, broke-down or not. Your survival is wasted. All of those men who died in a goddamned war that should never have started. You're throwing your life away on that airhead tramp who's only interested in you for what you can give her.

"You think about that brother, before you go throwing away a woman that wants to spend her life loving you. You need a giver, you miserable bastard. That lousy bitch you've been fucking is a taker."

There was dead silence as Joe stood there, glaring furiously at Nick.

"Fuck your computer," Joe said. "I'm out."

Chapter Fourteen

Second Chances (Go for It)

It was late morning and Sarah was lying on her sofa with Maxine on her tummy. The two of them were watching a movie that held neither of their interest. Sarah was looking at Nick's photo on her phone.

This is bullshit. I love this man, I want to spend the rest of my life with him, and I'm fucking lying here on the couch instead of fighting for what I want.

What the hell is the matter with me?

She pulled up her class roster and searched for Nick's address in Durham. *Do I even know whether he'll be home? No. But I've got to at least try. It's less than a half-hour from Cary to Durham. Get up, Sarah.*

The weather was mild to warm today, so she slipped on a pair of white capris and a navy-blue tank top with white sandals. She also decided on a Plan B. *If he's not home, I'll try again tomorrow. If he's not there today, I'll just swing over to Sandling Beach in Falls Lake State Recreation Area and enjoy the view while I do some yoga.* She tossed the important stuff from her purse into her beach bag, left the TV on for Maxine, and told her she could be in charge.

Maxine gave her the fisheye. "Don't give me that look. I'll be home in time to feed you."

Sarah had no sooner backed out of her driveway than she was struck by a thought. *Nick knows your car. Try not to look like you're stalking him, Sarah.* So, she drove over to Enterprise and rented a little economy Nissan for one day. She also pulled into a Dunkin Donut and got a large coffee to go while she was at it.

There were two cars parked in front of Nick's townhouse in Durham. One was his. The other one had just pulled up and a brunette got out, carrying a department store shopping bag. The brunette rang the bell. As she waited for the door to be answered she held her left hand up and admired the big ass diamond engagement ring that sparkled insanely in the sunlight.

A moment later the door opened, and brunette threw herself in Nick's arms. The door closed with the brunette inside. Sarah sank into her car seat and stared straight ahead.

Christ sakes, are you serious?

Well. We certainly resolved that quickly, didn't we? Apparently, I was easily replaceable.

Shit. That actually hurts. Well... damn.

She started the car and drove away. As she drove, Sarah groped in the beach bag on the passenger seat looking for a tissue and found that she had instead latched onto the napkin upon which the attractive Joe Anderson had written the big number two and his e-mail address.

She actually laughed through her tears. Sarah carefully slipped the napkin back in her bag, sniffed, and continued rummaging around until she found the little plastic tissue package instead.

"Well, it's not like you don't have an attractive alternate, eager to take Nick's place, Sarah," she told herself as she dried her eyes.

When she arrived at the recreation area, she grabbed her beach bag and headed for a fairly deserted section of lakefront Sandling Beach. Weekdays were pretty quiet, so she could take advantage of the solitude and try to gather her wits about her. Seeing Nick with his arms around the brunette had really hit her like a ton of bricks. Actually, it had damn near knocked the wind right out of her sails.

Sarah spread her large towel on the sand, set the beach bag on a corner of it, then sat down. She gazed out at the massive 12,000-acre reservoir. The tree-lined view was beautiful, of course, but she found herself struggling to come to grips with this new reality.

Sarah began with the Gate Pose, then segued into Tree Pose, Warrior One Pose and Warrior Two Pose, then stopped, inhaled deeply and looked up at the sky.

Is this truly it? Sarah wondered. *It felt so right between us. It actually still feels right in my heart, so that's what I don't understand. Maybe I've just totally gone round the bend.*

Sarah sighed again, then sat on the towel and gracefully slipped into Sphinx Pose followed by Extended Puppy pose, holding twenty seconds for each yoga pose.

***

"Did you go out to lunch with Joe?" Rachel asked Nick.

He shook his head. "Decided I wasn't hungry. Actually, I could use some fresh air.

"I was thinking about taking a drive over to the state park and going for a walk along the beach and the lakefront. Did you want to come with me?" he asked politely although he hadn't really wanted company. What he really wanted was to be able to do some thinking.

"Oh, all right," she said, not all that enthusiastic, but figuring that doing what he wanted would give her another chance to lobby for the lavish wedding she was bound and determined to have, whether he wanted it or not. "Oh, wait. I'll follow you there in my car. I have to run by Kendra's house for a minute when we're through."

Nick and Rachel had parked their cars at the opposite end of the parking lot which meant they started walking in Sarah's direction but from the far end of the beach. Flo had eagerly hopped out of the car. Walking along the beach was one of her favorite things. She was off leash, but she knew to stay close.

As the two of them walked along the beach, Rachel had begun haranguing Nick about having a lavish wedding. With a smile on his face, he humored her, urging her to explain why a big wedding was so important to her, getting her to explain in detail exactly what she was going to want in the way of gowns and flowers, the venue, and the date. He let it all go in one ear and out the other. The dawning of common sense had begun when he ran into Joe at the mall and Rachel had been looking at displays in the jewelry store window. It had hit him in stages. The first was when Joe had correctly identified Rachel as a gold digger, before he even knew who she was. The second was the feeling of blind, jealous rage that Nick had experienced when Joe implied, he and Sarah were dating. It took every ounce of self-control he had not to deck Joe, right then and there.

The third was the impatience, the underlying hostility, the resentment he sensed in Rachel, and the fact that she barely bothered to conceal her dislike of Flo. Of course, the feeling was mutual. Flo made no secret of the fact that she heartily hated Rachel's guts. Flo had always been an excellent judge of character.

All of these things had been going through his mind, even as he shopped for a suitably garish diamond engagement ring. He had wondered if receipt of the ring would mitigate any of her hostility, or her naturally acquisitive nature. Certainly not from what he'd seen so far. It had been an interesting experiment in human nature however, he thought.

Of course, feelings were still important, and he felt it necessary to let Rachel down gently.

He was still trying to figure out the best way to do that, when suddenly Flo stood stock still, put her nose in the air, sniffing something that had grabbed her attention. Before he even had a chance to react Flo took off at a dead run, something she had been trained never to do.

"What the *fuck? Flo! Flo, brace, brace, brace!*" She totally ignored him and kept on running, hell-bent for leather.

"Wait here!" he told Rachel and took off running after Flo. The damp sand at the edge of the water made running easier for him for some reason. He didn't lose his balance and he didn't fall. But what he registered as he grew closer scared the living daylights out of him. It looked as if Flo had knocked some poor person down and was actually mauling them.

"Oh my God, oh my God, *no Flo, no! Brace, Flo, brace, brace, brace!*"

He literally threw himself on top of the dog, grabbed her around the middle and bodily rolled her off of her victim, then rolled back over to determine the extent of the damage. Instead, he found himself lying face to face with Sarah. A wildly excited Flo, thrilled that Nick had apparently wanted to play-wrestle, had scrambled to her feet, raced around the other side of the towel and was now snuggling with Sarah for all she was worth.

Sarah had instinctively thrown her arms around Nick, and he'd instantaneously responded. "I will never let you go again, Sarah," he gasped, as he kissed her passionately.

"I swear to God I will never ever let you go; I love you with all my heart," he told her.

The two of them looked into each other's eyes and began laughing. "Took you long enough," she teased.

"Yeah, but I'm here, aren't I?" he said, still winded from his run. He laughed, then leaned over and kissed her again.

"How on earth did you find me?" she asked.

"I think Flo smelled your perfume. You're family. You belong with us. And if you'll have me, I plan to make that legal, damn near immediately," he said quietly.

Rachel made her entrance about two seconds later, wide-eyed and seriously pissed. "Excuse me? What the *fuck* do you think you're doing?" she shrilled at Nick.

"Uhhh..." Nick hadn't quite been prepared for this particular eventuality, but Rachel promptly relieved him of that responsibility.

"Well, it certainly didn't take you very long to start cheating on *me,* you son of a bitch!" she screamed hysterically.

"*I hate you.* I hate it when you fall. I hate your stupid fucking *dog,* and here's some news for you, buddy, I'm keeping this ring. It's *mine* and you can't have it back!"

Nick simply couldn't help himself.

"Mazel tov," he said calmly, and Sarah burst into gales of laughter.

Thoroughly enraged, Rachel whirled and stalked off.

"Oh jeez, Nick, I'm so sorry honey," Sarah said. "She's probably going to go hock the thing. They won't give her anywhere near what you paid for it. She'll be lucky to get half of what you spent."

"In that case she'll probably get about five hundred bucks, and as far as I'm concerned it was worth every penny of five hundred dollars to get rid of her."

"You bought her a *fake* engagement ring?" Sarah said, aghast.

"Well, no, not exactly. The semi-mount was real. The solitaire was a CZ. I've had her number for a while. I was just trying to figure out a diplomatic way to end it."

"This wasn't it, honey."

Chapter Fifteen

(And Then What Happened?)

It was a small military wedding, complete with sword arch and dress uniforms.

Ed Samuels and Big Lou jointly walked the bride down the aisle.

Joe Anderson was Nick's best man.

Flo wore flowers and a short veil, and was Sarah's maid of honor.

Nick's entire family attended the wedding, and as a wedding gift, Ed formally adopted Sarah, officially making her his daughter.

Sarah and Nick jointly exercised the option to purchase the house Sarah had been renting.

Nick narrated the newest graphic novel by their neighbors Sean Gallagher and Kyle Brewer at no charge, and with that book as a sample of his work, along with referrals from the guys, Nick was able to start his own company, doing audio book narration.

Nick and Sarah converted the small studio apartment above the detached garage into a recording studio, and the business became very successful.

Sarah's new course was extremely well received, as was her textbook. The university gave her a raise.

Nick was eventually able to fly a plane again, and Sarah earned her private pilot's license.

Nick's nightmares gradually became more manageable, and he was able to stop most of his medications with no ill effects. His home life was stable, and he was dearly loved.

Nick and Sarah adopted a perfectly adorable kitten, and an annoyed Maxine took a dump in Nick's shoe.

Lisa Wilford is a longtime resident of sunny South Florida. She and her husband, who is her best friend, share their home with Blue, their beloved Weimaraner-Pit. *Moving Forward* is Lisa's second book.

Printed in the USA
CPSIA information can be obtained
at www.ICGtesting.com
CBHW020719040224
4024CB00032B/65